knock three times
and ask for attila

knock three times and ask for attila

JAMEY GITTINGS

Attila Press
38242 Palo Colorado Road
Carmel, CA 93923

Paperback ISBN-13: 978-1-7923-5756-5

Visit our website at www.attilapress.com

Printed in the United States of America

ALSO BY JAMEY GITTINGS

On the Eradication of Smallpox and the Intractability of Raccoons
Meat of the Horse

For Daughter Briana and all her sisters & brothers

For Ronnie Rappaport
First contact; childhood friend

And for Dr. Sidney Bijou
your fingerprints are throughout

Apologia

The author admits to taking some liberties with the range of IQ scores attributed to the WAIS intelligence test. It was done to avoid a necessary technical treatment that would only have distracted from the story. In this case, simplicity trumped precision. My apologies to David Wechsler.

Disclaimer & Claimer

What follows is a work of fiction with respect to characters and plot, but the context and milieu represent the true state of affairs as I have seen them. With respect to the characters, three were inspired by real people. The narrative makes no attempt at presenting their actual details or accurately assessing their histories or actions. I have, in all but a few instances, made a conscious attempt to exclude these from the narrative. The instances that have crept into the story are presented allochronically (out of time); I have taken great liberties with time. I leave it to discerning readers of varied backgrounds to identify the sources of my inspiration. In doing so, however, he or she will gain little illumination.

In the story, I use a number of politically insensitive terms for individuals with mental retardation; I make no apology. To do less is to imply conditions are better than they are. As the narrator of the tale writes, "My penchant for using politically incorrect language, such as Mongoloid, feeb, moron, retard, and tard, is an active and cynical heuristic to not mitigate our position in history."

Phase I

Beginning

1

Bad Mr. 21

I wake up on this morning and close my eyes against the sun. What I see, in the red-and-black background, is the long tunnel of a hallway with what seems to be an infinity of doors, side by side, on both sides of the hall getting smaller as they stretch into the distance like railroad tracks.

I have seen this image many times upon waking, but on this morning, I know intuitively what the doors represent—they are the days of my life. Hardly a stretch into infinity, but a significant distance representing my thirteen years. I may have been vaguely aware of this before, but today I know I can look behind any door and retrieve the memories and feelings from that day. I open one to test this out; it's my fourth birthday party, and Mom and Dad are still together. It's at a park with big buildings all around it, and a white tall thin tower pointing into the sky. There are balloons, presents, and a cake on a folding table set out on the grass, and there are lots of children running around, screaming in delight. Almost all of them have round faces, slanty eyes, small button noses, and somewhat slack mouths. They all, both boys and girls, look a lot like me. There are a few children who don't look like me, but most do. I know all of their names.

I shut the door and open my eyes. I am fully awake now. I'm at my father's house in my bedroom, the translucent curtains are pulled back, and the windows are open—I always keep them open. Baseball pennants are tacked on the wall, as is a poster of Yogi Berra, my father's all-time favorite. Baseball is one of the loves of his life. A whiteboard calendar on which upcoming events are written in black marker hangs on the wall. I walk downstairs and find my father eating cereal and reading the newspaper at the dining room table. He looks over the paper, smiles, and says, "Good morning, Mason, did you sleep well?"

"Yeah," is my monosyllabic response. On this morning, I do not speak with the vocabulary that I'm writing with now. But my mind is working. I walk around the table and hug him. This is our morning routine, and he hugs me back warmly. I know that my father loves me even more than baseball. But this morning I keep hugging him and look to what I now know is the masthead of the newspaper. "Whaz that say?" I ask, pointing. My father looks at me, surprised by the question.

"It says *Washington Post*, it's the newspaper I work at, that I write for," he says in his precise and formal way. "Washington is the city we live in, even though our house is in a place called Georgetown. But that's a little confusing. You don't have to worry about that." My father is unusually flustered. "Post, well, it means mail, but, but here it means," he hesitates, "newspaper. Washington newspaper." I move across the table to my cereal bowl, and as I munch my granola, I look at him closely, for perhaps the first time. He's tall and thin, wears tortoise shell round glasses, sports grey slacks, a white shirt with a red tie, and is enclosed in a grey sport coat. He is cleanshaven, his blond hair cut short—shorter than mine. (My hair is always kept long to mitigate the somewhat odd shape of my head.)

I continue to look at him, taking him in. He seems uncharacteristically ill at ease under my stare that continues to seek information. This morning I have so many questions.

"Your mother is coming to pick you up to take you to that doctor again," he says with a slightly critical edge to his voice.

"Ah huh," I say. My mother is taking me to a doctor whom I have visited once before. My mother and father don't live together, and haven't since my seventh birthday. They interact civilly but without warmth; at this point in their history, they come together only around issues about me.

That's why it was unusual when a few days ago they had a terrible fight, with yelling and crying. My father at one point even drove his fist down hard on a table. "I won't have my son take part in an experimental study, Marilyn."

"It's only experimental because this is the first time it's been systematically tried. The science is well established, and the results are promising."

"What you're saying by this is that you don't love our son as he is, that he's not good enough without trying to modify him—make him better." This is where Dad struck the table and Mother started to cry. Mother cried for a few minutes, then spoke slowly, controlling her words.

"That's a cruel thing to say, William. It's manipulative and untrue. It's analogous to sending a child to college rather than trade school. It does not mean if he goes to trade school that he's less of a person, only that by college you are making a commitment to his potential. If that's not possible it's all right, but if it is, I think it's criminal to withhold the opportunity. You of all people should know this—should value this. Anyway, it's a moot point, the court gave me the sole custody of Mason at the time of the divorce, you didn't seem so passionate about his condition then. We have always shared Mason, but the custody has been mine, and I am going to have him participate, and that's final." Mother then left and Dad was quiet for a long time. I listened to their interactions, reacting to the emotions contained in their exchanges, but could not comprehend their meaning. I've had to open one of my doors for that.

On the day after the fight, we left from my father's house to a place called the National Institute for Health. It is a large series of buildings with which Mother seemed familiar. We went to an office where a few children who looked like me waited with their parents, sometimes both, most often just one. I wondered if the children with one parent had experienced a fight to get there.

One by one, the children were called through a door and went inside along with their parents. Since we arrived last, all of the other children were gone by the time we are called. "Mason Free," the lady at the door called my name, and we went inside to a little room where I was met by a Dr. Malone, who was smiley and spoke a bit too loudly. "Hi, Mason, I'm Dr.

Malone." I shook his hand. The lady who called my name was also there and held a syringe, like they give you your flu shot with. "You're not afraid of injections, are you?" The jocular doctor asked the rhetorical question, not waiting for an answer. I didn't know what injections were, but I figured they must be shots—shots, my word for both the injection and the implement that does the injecting. I nodded, wordlessly saying "Yes, I am not afraid of injections." I suppose it didn't matter anyway because the doctor continued his jolly narration. The lady, with what I took to be the injection, passed it to the doctor.

"You may think of this as a machine gun, or a bazooka," he said, chuckling to himself as he held it up for me to see, "and it is the weapon we use to kill Bad Mr. 21. You see Mason, you have an enemy inside of you that has been causing you a great amount of distress, and we are about to kill him, not all at once, mind you, but with a series of bazooka blasts over a couple of months. You don't mind that, do you?" I nodded to indicate "Yes, I do mind that," but nobody paid attention. If I could have understood what he was saying at the time, I would have been terrified. Enemies in my body that needed to be killed with multiple bazooka blasts? I would need a number of door openings to make sense of all this, but that would come later.

The doctor spoke to my mother, "Mrs. Free..."

"Ms." said my mother.

"What?"

"Ms., not Mrs. I'm no longer married."

"Ms. Free," continued the doctor, sounding slightly perturbed, "the injection, we believe, will neutralize the extra chromosome, and decrease some of its effects."

"How many factors will it affect, doctor?"

"We won't know until the completion of the study, but the therapy has shown promising results. This study will go a long way toward answering a variety of questions. As you are aware, in addition to the injections, the children will be observed and tested in our behavioral clinic to monitor ongoing progress and cognitive development; internal medicine will screen and evaluate physical changes."

This was how it started. The door openings would help me make sense of much of what followed.

2

The Playgroup

The day I've just reported is an account of the first day of my participation in the study and my introduction to Dr. Malone. To continue with my second day: With breakfast over, I complete the ritual of organizing and packing my backpack, important, since it determines in whose house I will be residing for the next number of days. I have lived in two houses since shortly after my seventh birthday.

I am waiting by the front door to respond to the honk that signals my mother's arrival and prevents the need for my parents to interact. My mother is a government appointee to the U.S. Department of Education in the area of special education, but I do not know this at the time. I greet her this morning with: "*Washington Post* means Washington newspaper. Washington is the place where we live, even though our house is in Georgetown. Post means mail, too." She looked at me for a moment with her mouth open, and that resolves into a broad smile. She giggles slightly and gives me a hug.

"Today you will be starting your playgroup," my mother says, using her word for behavioral clinic, "after your shot." I liked that she used a word with which I am familiar.

The injection follows the same pattern as the previous one, with Dr. Malone's spirited account of bazookas and Bad Mr. 21, and me grunting perfunctory responses to his prattle. This time, however, instead of returning to the car and my school, we go down the elevator to the basement where we pass through glass double doors into what appears to be a large classroom with a lot of different areas: places with groups of tables, some with little cubicles with spaces for only two people facing each other, areas with carpet and big pillows surrounded by low cases filled with books and games, areas with circles of chairs of varied numbers. Colorful posters adorn the walls— kittens, puppies, and smiling children playing on grass. Surrounding the entire room is a band of mirrors about a meter wide and the same height above the floor. Throughout the room, dangling from the ceiling, are things I now know to be microphones. There are no windows in the room, but it is well lighted and cheery.

As usual, we're late, or at least the last to arrive. We move to a circle of chairs where about fifteen children and two adults sit. Some of the children I have seen before at the doctor's office, but the adults are new to me. My mother walks me over to a chair, pats me on my shoulder, then leaves. "Welcome, Mason," says the woman with brown hair. The adults are both women.

"Hi," I say, in an upgrade from "huh."

"We are here today to get to know each other," says the blonde-haired woman. "We are all taking part in an important cooperation," her word for study, "that will be a good thing for everyone here. Before we get started on our structured activities, we want to learn all of our names. My name is Sally, and we'll go around the circle this way." She looks to the child to her right. "What is your name, dear?"

The girl mumbles something that sounds like "Uh".

"Very good, Mary," the blonde woman announces. As we move through the circle, each child ventures an approximation of their name. A wide range of fidelity is exhibited within the group. Some, however, remain silent, and Sally announces their name to the group and moves on. When the circle comes around to me, "Mashon," I say with a realization that this isn't exactly my name but is close enough for this group. I'm near the end. The brown-haired woman who is last says her name is Theresa.

Theresa directs us to where we need to be next, and the two women assist us in getting to our predetermined stations. At each station, or center, as they call them, is at least one new adult who looks younger than Sally and Theresa. I'm directed to a cubicle designed for two people to work in privacy, but two chairs are set on one side of the table facing Ted, the adult. I sit next to a girl named Holly. She is about my age, and has curly really yellow hair. I wonder if her parents keep her hair long to hide an odd-shaped head like mine. I look, and her head appears fine to me. Holly was number one on the name fluency exercise, enunciating perfectly and with a confidence not displayed by any of the rest of us.

Our teacher, Ted, has a book with a list of words and asks us to read them. I know very few. Holly, however, knows almost all of them. Ted writes furiously on a clipboard. The cubicle is actually a bit too small for two people on one side, but it feels nice to be this close to Holly. Occasionally, we bump our arms and shoulders into each other, and I even engineer some of these. The session is coming to an end, and I don't want Holly to think I'm stupid, so I say to Ted: "I know how to write *Washington Post*."

"You do?" says Ted, who hands me the clipboard and a pencil.

I can now read *Washington Post*, but I've never written it. I'm worried that I've overreached, but I look at Holly, take the pencil and write out a scrawly "*Washington Post*."

"Great," says Ted, and Holly, who seems impressed, smiles at me and giggles.

My mother is waiting for me at the mouth of the glass double doors. "How did it go?" she asks.

"Great," I bubble. It was the first time I had ever used the word, and I wonder where it came from.

3

Phonics

After the third injection and the first play group, I'm into my second week of the study. We're meeting twice a week, and I'm excited to be experiencing some changes. I'm more aware of my surroundings and how I interact with them. I have an anticipation like an impending spring after a long winter. I'm also becoming interested in the printed word, paying attention to written material, newspapers and magazines mostly, since they seem to be everywhere. I'm reinforcing my emerging tendencies by increasing my facility with door openings. I open the door that contains my last few hours and review the words I've been tested on, and those addressed by Holly. Although I was only tested and not taught, I know them all, what they mean, how to read them, and given my recent experience with *Washington Post*, probably how to write them. My mother continues to give me sideways looks as I ask her about the words that appear on billboards and shop signs as she drives me to school.

Four days later, I'm back in the cubicle sitting close to Holly. Holly begins on her list of words and she does well, but misses more than she did on her first day. I pay attention to her responses as well as Ted's corrections. "Good job, Holly!" says Ted. Then: "Your turn, Mason." He gives me the same list as I had in the last session. I'm asked the words and get them all correct, and he checks the words on his list and gives me a long look. "Did you study these words?" he asks me. "Uh uh," I say, and I look at Holly, then amend my answer to "No." It's maybe a lie. I don't share my multiple sessions of door openings, besides I don't yet have the words to explain my process. He scribbles a few lines on his clipboard, hesitates, then says to himself, "I wonder." He excuses himself and goes to Theresa, where they have an animated conversation. I can't hear what they are saying, but at the end Theresa mouths what looks like "go ahead."

Ted returns and quizzes me on the cards he had just presented to Holly. I look carefully at each and read back the words to Ted's astonishment. "Very good. Really good, Mason." I look over at Holly, who is observing this and she smiles at me, and I smile back. Ted works his way to the end of the cards and again excuses himself and confers with Theresa, who has moved closer and is observing us.

"Go to the phonics protocol," she directs.

"I'm going to change some things up," Ted says as he puts the piles of cards away. He takes out a sheet of paper encased in plastic, with uppercase alphabet letters. The letters are mostly colored blue, five of them are yellow, and the letter Y is in red.

"This is the alphabet. Can you tell me the name of each letter?" I go first and get about a quarter of them correct, the legacy of seven years of school. Then he turns to Holly, who gets them all right, followed by "Very good, Holly." Ted then asks me to repeat the exercise, and this time I also get them all right. Holly looks at me and giggles. I experience a feeling that I will later learn is described with the metaphor *my heart leaps*.

Ted asks me to repeat the exercise then says, "100 percent." Loud enough for Theresa to hear, as she's now observing attentively. We both repeat this instructional sequence with a sheet of lowercase alphabet letters. The results are exactly the same, though I do score higher than the first time since a lot of the lowercase letters look like the uppercase ones. He then pulls out another sheet with uppercase letters beside lowercase ones, and we both get them all correct the first time. He looks at Theresa, who nods at him.

Ted then picks up the sheet with both upper- and lowercase letters and says, "Each of these letters has a name which you both have demonstrated that you know. In addition, every letter has a sound, and some letters have more than one sound. Let's look at A," he continues cheerfully. "A is both the letter's name and the letter's sound, like in the word Amy. We have a girl in our group whose name is Amy." He pauses, and we look back without any emotion, though we can tell that Ted is happy about what he's saying. "But A has another sound, ahh, like in the word animal. When you read a word you either read it directly with your memory, where you read it as a whole, or you use the sounds of the letters strung together to sound out the word." Ted elongates the words "sound out," as if he's chewing them. Holly and I just stare at him through this confusing recital. Ted looks nervously over at Theresa, then courageously marches on.

"When we read our words earlier today, you probably used both methods—ways," he amends, "to read them. We call reading from memory as whole word, or sight word reading, and we call reading by sounding out words, reading by phonics. Can you say phonics?" Holly says it perfectly, and I say something that sounds more like phoenix—and we continue to stare. Ted again seems a little nervous and says, "Good. Let's try a few more examples." Theresa clears her throat loudly, and Ted looks over anxiously.

"Baseline." Theresa utters the single word.

"Baseline, right," says Ted, who sits upright in his chair, squares his shoulders, and retrieves the alphabet sheet. Ted begins his queries with me. I do not yet know the meaning of baseline, but he's catching on to the effect of me following Holly, and he moves to protect the integrity of his baseline.

All my words are obviously sight words, as my only correct response is for Aa. Holly, however, knows a good number of the answers Ted is looking for; he writes furiously on his clipboard.

"Can I try again?" I ask, having just added to my sight-word vocabulary.

"No.," says the beleaguered Ted sharply. Then softening his response, he says, "The session's almost over."

Ted excuses himself and walks over to Theresa. Holly and I look at each other, smiling silently until the group members are called to the large circle of chairs where we begin each day's activities. Sally tells us we have all been doing nice work and how proud she is of all of us. She then asks us to repeat the name-giving activity and we go around stating to the group our names.

It seems to me that the group is more successful this time around. Mary, who previously gave her name as "Uh," now pronounces Mary perfectly. The younger teachers stand outside of the circle and write energetically. "Now one more thing before we leave," Sally says. "We would like you to go around the circle to your right and say the name of each group member you can remember." She has to repeat these directions twice before the first person next to Theresa can correctly follow the instructions. A girl named Hilda gets about five of the 17 souls sitting around the circle correct, and we move on. People at the end of the line have a distinct advantage over the ones who go first. The success rate ranges from between only themselves, since you count yourself, to about 12 to 14. Holly and I are second to last and last, respectively, so I have 15 trials to learn everyone's name. By the time the exercise comes around to us, Holly only misses one with a score of 16, and I miss none. Pretty poor baseline, I realize only later.

4

The Swinging Monkey

On the way home, I continue to ask my mother the meaning of words I see, and to read the words on storefronts, buses, trucks, and billboards. At one point, she says under her breath, "It's only three weeks…"

'What is, Mama?" I've rarely called her Mama, and at the next stop she hugs me tightly and says, "Dr. Malone and the playgroup." Then, under her breath, "I wonder what your father thinks of all this." I've been less direct with demonstrating my milestones in front of my father, who, I realize, has his objections. That evening I ask him to teach me to read. He is indulgent of my request, though I realize he has limited expectations. He decides to use the *Washington Post* as the major medium of instruction. Most of the teaching takes place at the breakfast table before I leave for school or get picked up by my mother for the playgroup, or after dinner. We progress quickly from the comics to stories my father selects from the interior of the paper. One is about a barking dog that awakens a family with two young children whose apartment has a gas leak. The roused parents awaken groggily to extract the family, call the fire department, and save the day. I like this story, so my father cuts out the article and sets it aside, and we use it over the next couple of days. After the first day I can read all the words but pretend to struggle for the sake of my father. His teaching method is to read it with me, select specific words, then underline them for future review. Up to now I've used only the sight-word method, but my mother returns me to my father's home with a new word—phonics.

After dinner, we go back to the dog story and I get all the underlined words right. My father has gradually been getting used to my increasing proficiency. "Good, Mason, that's impressive," he says, taking off his reading glasses and looking at me.

He's about to select some new words to learn when I say, "Dad, have you ever heard of phonics?"

"Ah, yes…" he answers haltingly, looking closely at me again.

"Can I learn to read with phonics?" I ask. "It's a way of sounding out words instead of memorizing them."

"Well, yes, we can try it." My father hasn't thought of phonics for many years; after an awkward and ineffective half-hour, he says, "I think if you're interested in phonics, you can use your tablet. It will do a better job of teaching than I can." I hadn't thought of my tablet since I've started working with Dr. Malone and the playgroup, and opening doors. It's like a little TV that I have used to play cartoons and look at animal videos. I had never considered it as a teacher. "Go get it for me," he says.

I bring down my tablet, and my father takes it. He taps in the word phonics and a word I don't yet know—programs. Taps it twice more and a picture of a smiling monkey swinging on a rope appears, along with the words "Swinging on Phonics." I know the words "on" and "Phonics." "Phonics," from Ted and the playgroup, "on", from a group of cards my mother has been working on with me that identify the most frequently used words in the English language. Words like *the, a, in, on, that* are all over written material. I ask my father what the other word is and he says, "Swinging. The monkey is swinging on a vine." A vine, not a rope. A vine, I'm told, is a plant that lives in jungle trees. "It means, I believe, doing well with phonics," my father says, sighing.

The next half hour is directed at teaching me how to move around the tablet and the phonics program. I can tell that my father is beginning to take my intellect more seriously as he quizzes me on what he's just taught. My facility comes too quickly, and I think it makes him nervous. It's a challenge to his commitment against change. It also makes me nervous, or even a little afraid. I still don't fully understand the inchoate feelings and emotions that accompany my emerging facility with words, but they fill me with caution.

I sleep very little this night, using my tablet to move through letters, sounds, rules, and exceptions, taught by the swinging monkey, so that between phonics and my mother's cards, I can read almost anything by early morning. I say *read* to describe my oral handling of written words.

5

Reading and Reading

I've referred to my learning to recognize words and duplicate their pronunciation as reading, but I'm not sure my progress is genuine reading. Perhaps it is learning to read, but not reading itself. In this process, I realize that I am the teacher and the student, both. I think reading describes an intimate relationship between the one doing the writing and the one doing the reading, and this is decidedly not what I am doing, certainly not in the beginning. What I am doing is more akin to breaking a code populated with unfamiliar arrangements of letters, words, and other little marks I don't yet know the names of.

Indeed, I was breaking a code like in the story *The Gold Bug*, by Edgar Allan Poe, that my father read to me when I was about ten years old. He was reading it to himself in a spacious easy chair, and I snuggled in next to him and he just started reading out loud. I couldn't understand most of the words, but it is still the most gentle moment I've ever spent with my father. The story was about breaking a code on a treasure map and the subsequent finding of the treasure. I opened a door to relive the experience.

I've mentioned door openings previously but have not explained the process. Somehow, early on in my memory, the days of my life were apportioned and marked by a series of doors stretching into the distance. These doors were my way of conceptualizing my history when I closed my eyes, but what lay behind the doors remained inaccessible. With the beginning of the gene therapy program, each day was retrievable in its entirety; I could relive the experience. It was like a do-over in my personal history. I couldn't change anything in the memory, but I could slow it down, or even stop it, so I could analyze what was happening, look up words in my Oxford (more on this later), and make sense of it. But I could do this only once, and once I left the memory the door was gone. My memory of it was only that, a memory. The doors were more like a vault, and once I'd extracted what was within, the vault disappeared. It was, however, a tremendous gift and allowed me to replace a fuzzy recollection with a precise memory, analyze it, and thus augment my personal history. As I opened more doors they disappeared; the railroad track became shorter as my memory became dominant.

So, I revisited *The Gold Bug*. I found the correct door and relived the experience, and it was much as I remembered it. This time my vocabulary was better, though there were many words I still did not understand. The breaking of a code leading to treasure seemed an apt metaphor for my current reading process, and I was hopeful that the result would be similar to the end of the story.

I suspect that writing is more intimate than a conversation. I've tried to write letters to Holly, but my emotions always outstripped my pathetic vocabulary and limited verbal fluency. Anyway, back to reading, with a cautionary tale of swallows.

When I was around ten, about the time of *The Gold Bug*, a family of swallows built their mud nest on the eave that overhangs the east window of my bedroom, and I could observe them while lying in my bed. I watched the adult pair assemble their nest, little by little, with mouthfuls of mud, building the scalloped walls layer by meticulous layer. I watched the nest grow bigger until they laid their eggs, though I didn't actually see the eggs being laid. I watched them sitting on the nest protecting their eggs, sometimes alone taking turns, sometimes together. I watched as the chicks were born, six of them, crowded into the small mud saucer until they grew so large that the nest could barely contain them. I watched as their parents relentlessly fed their greedy open yellow beaks, as I watched the young ones became fully feathered and perched tentatively on the edge of their earthen home flapping their wings. I saw as the first intrepid child stepped off into the air, managing only to glide down into the garden where our cat, Franklin, had been waiting for days.

I wish I could say that the youngster found his wings and soared into the sky just ahead of Franklin's pounce, but I can't—Franklin devoured him in a heartbeat. His brothers and sisters were more prudent; they waited longer and mastered the air, evading the ever-vigilant Franklin. I later thought that the flight of the first bird was a cautionary tale of trying to achieve something before you were ready. At the time of my first forays into reading and writing, I thought of that bird. I was aware of my expectation of what I wanted out of reading, like the awareness of the promise of the air was for the young swallow, but I wanted to be ready. So, I hesitated. Though I wrote a hundred letters to Holly, I never delivered one.

Reading, and later writing, became a transport for me, not just a way to accumulate information about the world, but a device for transforming my life into the lives of others where I could apprehend different sensibilities, insights beyond my own, and share the world with other beings.

I did go back to *The Gold Bug*, after the door opening, and reread the original story. It was still a bit too early—it was a difficult piece, but I navigated it with the help of the Oxford. Reading became like flying, and I always wished I could share the feeling with that precocious early bird.

6

Dictionaries

I can read the words, but I don't know what they mean. However, as I've said, it is a limited definition of reading. Here again the monkey swings to the rescue. A number of the words that I'm learning to read with the monkey's help are in blue. When I hit them with the little arrow I can move around, something called the Monkey's Dictionary appears, and it provides a short definition of the word. I am both elated and excited with the implications. It's fortuitous that it is a child's dictionary since I have to get definitions for some of the words in a definition. Initially, it's a slow process.

Another advantage of the monkey's dictionary is it says the word out loud, so I learn both the meaning and its pronunciation. It takes me another night to exhaust its contents. Two nights into my three-night stay at my father's house, I can read much of the English language, and I know the meaning of a lot of words, at least all the words in the brachiating simian's lexicon and on the 200 cards of my mother's most frequently used words.

It strikes me that I need a similar dictionary for my feelings and emotions, which are undergoing as much modification as my facility with words and language. None exists, however, and I'm left only with my unfolding experience.

I'm down early for breakfast, munching my granola on the last day of my stay with my father, and I read through the entire *Washington Post* before he arrives. It's merely a phonics exercise, since I can't understand any of the articles. There are too many words that I don't yet know the meaning of, and knowing the definitions of words doesn't automatically help with the concepts. But I can understand small parts of the stories, and this makes me happy. In the back section of the newspaper, I come across one with my father's picture and I read it. I can pronounce the words, but I can't understand any of it, my phonics skills far exceeding my understanding. When Dad arrives, I ask incautiously, "What does government mean?"

My father, who is sitting down, looks puzzled, stands back up, and stares at me; I realize I might have made a mistake. "Where did you hear that?"

"I read it in the *Washington Post*," I say, perhaps compounding my mistake.

"Where?" My father looks distressed.

"I was looking through the *Washington Post*, and, I saw your picture," I answer not telling the whole truth. "I read it under your picture."

"You... read it. How?" He stutters his question.

"Phonics," I smile. "Well," I say to shift the focus off me, "what does it mean?"

"Government," he says, adopting his formal voice, "is what manages a country. Allows it to function. People vote to have a few people run the government for the many." None of this makes any sense to me, and I continue to stare at him but am relieved that we've moved away from my reading. I feel I would have to use more caution in the future, not to make him nervous of my budding abilities. "Government is very complicated, people spend their whole lives trying to understand it." I want to ask what complicated means but think better of it, and munch my cereal until I hear my mother's horn, extracting me from the awkward situation. I get my backpack and kiss my father, who remains silent. I think, in the wake of my increasing understanding, that I fear my father's disapproval. I'm beginning to care, for the first time, what other people think of me, of how

I'm viewed in their eyes. I let this thought slip from my consciousness, as I run to my mother's waiting car.

7

___

The Parent Meeting

It's Monday, one of the playgroup days, but first we check in with Dr. Malone for another bazooka blast. My heart takes flight (another heart metaphor; I'm just beginning to understand the subtle power of metaphor), when I see Holly in the waiting room. But before I can go over and talk to her, she's called by the nurse, and she and a man who must be her father go inside the doctor's office. But we still smile at each other, and I say "hello," not "huh," not "hi." She doesn't say anything, but waves, and my heart leaps. I figure that I'll see Holly when she comes out, but the nurse calls us in first and puts us into an empty room, saying that the doctor will be in shortly. I don't know the word shortly, but I know the word short, and wonder if Dr. Malone will be smaller than the last time. No Holly and a small Dr. Malone don't make me happy.

Dr. Malone prances in, his normal size, but talks more to my mother than to me with a different vocabulary, sans machine guns and bazookas hitting their mark. "I'll see you at the parent meeting this morning," he says, and my mother says that she'll be there.

"What's a parent meeting?" I ask as we leave the office.

"The parents and the staff are all meeting this morning to review your progress." I don't understand the word "progress," but I'll figure it out when I open today's door. Doors have become a major mechanism of how I review and understand my new world. It's not quite a do-over, but it is a think-over.

We get to the playgroup room and there's a good crowd of people: all of our group, and all of their mothers and fathers. I see Dr. Malone and lots adults I've never seen. Some, like Dr. Malone, wear long white coats. There's our usual circle placed at the rear of the room, and rows of seats facing a long table with chairs around one side at the front. Our group and theirs are as far apart as they can be from each other. The rows of chairs have their back to our circle.

The four people in white coats sit down at the table. Sally sits down by the white coats, and other adults who I've never seen take their seats. Dr. Malone is in the center. Parents begin to fill the rows of chairs. Theresa calls our group together and tells us to form our circle and continue to learn each other's names, then leaves us to take her seat at the long table. For the first time, our group is all by itself.

8

On Our Own

We look at each other; everyone is silent until a small boy named Logan asks, "Anybody noticing any changes?" The bolder of us say yes or nod; the others just stare.

"I think Bad Mr. 21 is dying," I say. The others comprehend and nod.

"Can anyone here read?" Logan continues. Most nod their heads and say something affirmative—our little group is loosening up.

"Can you?" I ask Logan.

"Fuckin' A," answers Logan with a smile. "Learned to read with the motherfucking monkey."

"Is that the Swinging Phonics monkey?" I probe.

"Son of a bitchin' yes. That and the *Dictionary of Slang* I found in my father's library. Do you guys know that there are some words that you shouldn't say? I'm learning them all, and I'm going to use them, too." This seems to come as a surprise to all of us in the group, but we like Logan's animation. It's infectious.

"I used the F-word after I heard my brother use it. My mother slapped me, and told me not to say it again," says Mary in quite a step up from her name as "Uh" on our first day. All this is news to me.

"That's fucking lame, fucking bullshit," Logan replies.

Some of the group relate similar stories and reactions. "I'll tell you something else," says Logan, "Our parents are not completely comfortable about all the changes. I've caught my mother, the cunt bitch, looking at me strangely when I do, or say, something new. They're not to be trusted." This assessment helps to clarify some of my feelings of trepidation and my hesitation to be transparent with my father about my emergent intellect.

Other group members relay more stories, and I share my concerns about my father's tentative and less-than-welcoming responses. I don't yet know the word "suspicious," but suspicion is the operative feeling exhibited by our group and will become an obsession in my observations of our group's progress. However, this will ultimately play out, and we all agree to be more secretive with our progress and milestones. I share information about the tablet and the Swinging Phonics monkey, but not everybody has access to one.

Charles, one of the older boys, says that we need to find a way to meet without the presence of adults. I can hear the group at the table, and Dr. Malone is saying that the gene therapy is more effective than previously anticipated as demonstrated by the data gathered by behavioral clinic staff. The parents all nod and talk among themselves. The meeting is ending.

Consistent with our suspicions, we all agree to hold back on showing the extent of our progress, also to look for a way to meet as a group. Logan sees Sally and Theresa move toward our group. "Look, sharp people, the twats are coming," he says cheerfully. Between Logan and the adult meeting, I have a door to open and a date with my tablet's *Oxford Dictionary of the English Language*, of which I have made previous reference that has supplanted the monkey. It will be, for a while, the most influential book in my development.

9

The Social Group

On my way home, I give my mom a break from my constant barrage of questions about the meaning of words we pass. "Mama," I use the more enduring term and I see her smile, "I really like the boys and girls in my playgroup."

"That's wonderful, Mason," she says and puts her hand on my head.

"I liked the meeting we had without the grown-ups," I throw out the leading statement. "Could we have more meetings like that, with just us?"

My mother, I find out later, is a powerful government administrator who controls, among other things, the budget for the behavioral clinic. She gives me a long look and puts on her administrator's face. "That's an interesting idea, Mason. I, I think we can work something out. What you're asking for is a social group, to address your socialization and the development of your social relationships. Yeah, that's a good idea." She smiles and ruffles my hair again. Still the professional, she adds, "I'll call the other parents and I'm sure we can work something out." I know what "social" means, but "socialization" is another word for today's open-door review, along with most of the words used by Logan, and a few from Dr. Malone.

True to her word, my mother organizes a social group as part of what I now refer to as the study—Dr. Malone's word. I still have the old tablet at my father's house, but I have a new top-of-the-line laptop computer at my mother's. I have not taken the time to explore it and don't use it like my tablet. Throwing caution to the wind, I ask my mother to instruct me in its use. I don't experience the same nervous feelings with my mother as I do my father as she seems less judgmental—less threatened by my developing abilities.

I catch on quickly and can soon access the Internet, and there I find information on virtually anything. Most helpful is Logan's *Dictionary of Slang*, as many of the words are absent from the Oxford. There are writing programs that I use to reinforce the strides I'm making in my verbal fluency in the journal I keep of my day's revelations with respect to knowledge and language. Also, my emotional dictionary begins to gain some entries. I highlight these by placing them in a different color—red. One item states: *People's words don't always reflect what they mean. Often, they mean the opposite of what they say.* Another is: *People make decisions that are not always in their best interests.* Both of these are major steps forward to understanding the world I am finding myself in.

Previous to our first social group, I had overheard a conversation between my mother and Dr. Malone. It turned out that my mother was in charge of the study. "No," I heard her say, "I don't think we should do it at the clinic. It's a social group, it should be in a social setting. Yes, I realize that you could observe and record the meetings in the clinic, but that's not the point of a social group, now, is it?" She continues: "I've talked to the other parents, and we're all in agreement, and before you refuse again I would ask you to consider where your funding comes from." So, the matter was settled, and we met for the first time. And most importantly, in private. From the overheard conversation, I developed two things: a respect for the character of my mother, and a distrust of the motives of Dr. Malone and his playgroup setting, confirming earlier suspicions.

The meeting takes place at my mother's house in a basement room decorated by a previous owner that my mother has not yet bothered to change. It is fitted out as a rec room with a pool table upon which my mother has set out an array of chips, fresh vegetables, salsa, hummus, guacamole, popcorn, and finger sandwiches, a variety of soft drinks and juices, and a CD player with a number of CDs that currently is playing Smokey Robinson and the Miracles, an old CD of my mother's. Instead of chairs there are throw pillows, spread over an oriental rug, enough for twenty people. Most of our group is here, and I'm glad to see Holly among them. "Fucking good digs," says Logan, as he takes a handful of potato chips and sits down on a pillow. Holly and I talk a little about what our favorite things are, she says she likes kittens and elephants. I tell her I have a cat at my father's house, called Franklin, "Cats make my mother sneeze, so we don't have one here, but we have a dog named Adam Smith. He used to be my father's but my mother took him with her when they separated." I realize I've never been this chatty, but I can't stop myself—I'm so excited to be near Holly without Ted and the playgroup staff.

10

Mongoloid Defined

"What do you like?" she asks me.

"Going to the zoo with my mom, and going to baseball games with my dad. And I like Franklin," I say in my first expression of social awareness. Holly smiles, and my heart sings. Charles, the boy who originally suggested that we find a way to meet without adults, decides to take charge.

"Can everyone take a seat and we can get this meeting started?" Charles announces. Meeting? I thought this was a social group. The language fluency of our group certainly has blossomed since the first day name circle, I think. Mary, or Uh, as I continue to think of her, is holding an animated conversation with two other group members.

With some grumbling, we turn off Smokey and all take a seat on a pillow on the floor, arranging ourselves in an approximation of a circle. "What's the motherfucking agenda?" asks Logan. His monkey scholarship is certainly exceeding mine.

"Agenda?" I note sliently.

Charles continues, "We are meeting here to decide some important issues."

"Issues?" I'm impressed.

He continues. "We need to decide how to deploy ourselves."

"Deploy?" I really need the *Oxford*.

"We need to know how to behave around the adults. Something is happening that they're not prepared for."

"What do you mean?" I ask, using my nascent vocabulary.

"We are changing at an incredible rate. I'm now smarter than my parents and either of my brothers, and I keep learning."

"Fucking A," interjects Logan. "Last night my father, who's a motherfucking doctor, was trying to set up a new stereo. He fumbled with it for an hour without getting anywhere, so I took over and set it up in five minutes. I love the old cocksucker, but boy, is he dumb."

I know the word "dumb," since I've been called that by fellow students since kindergarten. The other one will need a door, and probably the *Dictionary of Slang*.

"Precisely my point," says Charles. "Unless you've missed it, we are all mongoloids, or more civilly, people with Down Syndrome."

"What's a Mongoloid?" echoes through the group. First, I've heard of it, I think, although through multiple door openings I realize both terms had been said around me myriad times—later, I realize, I've not been paying enough attention.

Charles continues bitterly, "We've lived our lives as retards, at least that's the consensus of everyone around us." I know the word "retard," however, having been defined by it over my brief lifetime. "The reason for this is an extra chromosome that we have and others don't." I've heard the word "chromosome" from conversations Dr. Malone has had with my mother during our bazooka blasts but have no clear idea of its meaning. Members look at each other blankly. "From my research," Charles continues, "we're all supposed to have 46 chromosomes, two each forming twenty-three pairs."

He continues, "Chromosome pairs are numbered from 1 to 23; 1 to 22 are autosomes, body chromosomes, and we all have them; then we have two sex chromosomes that determine whether we are boys or girls." Everyone is keenly attentive to Charles's narration.

"How do you know this?" I ask, impressed.

"Looked it up on my laptop. It's really easy," he says modestly. I'm beginning to like Charles.

"Another word for our condition is Trisomy 21, meaning we have three chromosomes for number 21." He pauses. "It's actually three chromosomes at number 22, the smallest chromosome. It was originally misidentified, but once it was named, it was too much trouble for the scientists to change it." Charles says this with disdain.

"Duplicitous motherfuckers," Logan says.

Charles nods at Logan and continues his remedial lecture. "Gene therapy, which is why we're all here, is a way to turn off the bad effects of the extra chromosome, and it seems to be working, allowing us to learn in giant steps. It seems to be working so well that we are not only as smart as typical people, but it's making us far smarter."

"That's why Dr. Malone says they're killing Bad Mr. 21," says a girl named Amy, the example of the long A in Ted's phonics lesson.

"Exactly, Amy, and I think our new condition may be a greater threat to us than was our retardation," says Charles ominously. "We all need to be careful what we show them about our emerging abilities."

"Why?" asks Holly.

"Look," says Charles, "we're labeled retarded because we're perceived as slow. That's what retarded means—slow or delayed. People—society— look down on us because they see us as lesser beings, and they treat us that way as well. What do you think will happen when they become lesser to us? Do you think they'll like that? Do you think they'll let it go on?" He closes with, "We all need to be careful."

Charles' reasoning successfully fosters a feeling of paranoia in our little group. It's a word I don't know at the time, but as our history progresses, paranoia is transformed into tangible fear. Some of the others share stories of how they have made parents, and family friends worried or upset with their newly achieved abilities. I share my account of my mother's conversation with Dr. Malone, and how he wanted to observe and record our social group.

"I've never trusted that verbose piece of shit," ejaculates Logan.

The girl named Hilda relates how she ran herself a bath for the first time; previously, her mother had done this for her since she could not be trusted around hot water. "I was about to enter the water and my mother comes into the bathroom and screams, she takes me by the hand and pulls me away. Rather than being relieved when she felt the water, she was upset and assumed I had just been lucky to run the correct temperature. She told me never to do it again; then she drained the tub and refilled it."

"We're almost at the end of our time here," Charles says, looking at his watch. I notice that he's the only one of us to be wearing a watch—the only one, perhaps, with a concept of time. Changing the subject, he asks, "How many of you have laptops?" About a third of us raise our hands. "Those of you who don't, need to try to get one. We need to be accessing the same websites, at least at first, until we all share a common knowledge. It's so much more effective a teacher than the behavioral clinic."

Amy suggests we should show bits of learning to demonstrate the effectiveness of the gene therapy, while keeping the major strides secret. We all murmur our agreement.

"Concentrate on those skills that will lead your parents to increase your independence, where you can do things by yourself, like drawing a bath or crossing a street," Charles recommends.

Before we disband, we share the websites that we should consult before our next meeting: these include the *Swinging on Phonics* monkey, the *Oxford* dictionary, and *Understanding Down Syndrome* by the Mayo Clinic, and we agree to look for other useful sites. We conclude our meeting to Logan's cheerful encouragement to "get a bitchin' laptop."

When my mother and a few other parents descend the stairs, we're all on our feet, and the Dixie Chicks are now on the CD player singing happily about the murder of a wife abuser. We munch on chips and finger sandwiches, and we talk energetically to each other, trying look like what we think a social group should look like.

11

Laptop Wars

There is a lot of information in Charles's account that was news to me. For one thing, I never knew that I was a Mongoloid, but I chalked it up to my cosmic lack of attention. After the social group, I go right to my laptop and key in "Mongoloid." First, I reach a website that describes the people and culture of Mongolia. Even though this makes little sense to me, I read through it all. It is very interesting, although confusing with respect to how I am related to these attractive and exotic people, who look nothing like me or anyone else in the social group. I am particularly interested in the part of their history that concerned the leadership of Genghis Kahn, who, in the fifth century, almost conquered the world and was directly responsible for making the B blood group ubiquitous. From Genghis Kahn, I am diverted to a website for Attila the Hun, who was quite the global warrior and who came a hair's breadth of worldwide domination centuries before Genghis. Attila was a Mongolian, before there was a Mongolia, but shared the same pedigree as Genghis. I am intrigued by the colorful Attila and resolve to learn more about him.

I exit these engaging, if irrelevant, websites to find *Mongoloid: A False and Demeaning Term for Down Syndrome*: an angry platform that indignantly clarifies my lack of relationship to the Mongolian people. A doctor in history of genetics had thought that I and my fellows' facial features resembled those of Mongolians. And, like trisomy 21, when the sloppy simile was exposed, it was too much trouble to rectify. The website also relates abuses of the term applied pejoratively to non-Down Syndrome people.

Charles' message to us all, in addition to stimulating my interest in gene therapy and related topics, alerts me to the importance of laptops in our future development. I am now learning to use it to solve specific problems. It is providing me with specific skills, as well as the ability to speak to myriad (my new word) deficits in my background. As I learn more, the laptop begins to take over the function of my door openings, at least in relationship to the present, although not to my past.

I thought of Charles's instruction to those without laptops to do what they could do to get one.

Mine was a good one, particularly in comparison with the tablet at my father's house. What about those other kids? Kids? Colleagues, a better term. What about my colleagues who don't have laptops? We are all like babies learning about our world, and about two thirds of us have a distinct disadvantage in this process.

I remember my mother's disagreement with Dr. Malone about the social group, as well as her considerable influence, and ultimate victory. I reach for my laptop and enter her name, and a website for the United States Department of Education appears.

The website highlights: Marilyn Free is an assistant Secretary of Education and the director of the Office of Special Education; she graduated with a master's degree in history from Georgetown University; was married and divorced from William Free, a conservative columnist with the *Washington Post*. The most notable part of the government website, for me, is a statement from my mother that she runs her office as a mother, not as an educational professional—for expertise, she hires special education professionals. A significant cornerstone of her administration is a number of grants to improve the lives and services of persons with specific handicaps. One recipient is a Dr. Connor Malone for a gene therapy approach to remediating Down Syndrome. "That's us!" I realize, and I read through his blurb on the website.

It's us in a nutshell, the Bad Mr. 21 injections and the playgroup. There's no mention of the social group.

I come away from all this with a new understanding of my mother and her power. At the next playgroup, we're all a little tentative, not sure how to react to the demands and requests of the staff. I'm more restrained in how I respond to Ted's instruction, and everyone seems to be a little nervous, but we get through the day seemingly without increased scrutiny or detection. As we wait for our parents to pick us up, Charles approaches each of us and asks what progress we've made in gaining access to a laptop. He's obviously discouraged by the answers and continues his encouragement to try. When my mother retrieves me, she says, "Mason, we need to stop at my office, there are a few things I need to attend to before I take you to school. I hope you don't mind."

I certainly don't mind. I've never much liked school, but after Bad Mr. 21's bazooka blasts, it has become excruciatingly boring. "No worries, Mama," I say. She looks at me and smiles and ruffles my hair. "Mama, do you think I'm getting smarter?"

She looks long at me at a traffic stop, and says earnestly, "Yes Mason, I think you really are." She laughs. "Yes, I think you are."

We take off in the heavy late morning Washington traffic. "You know that since you showed me how to use my laptop, it's helping me to gain intelligence." I use a word from my Down Syndrome websites. From my readings and the *Oxford*, intelligence seems to be the primary factor in our disability.

My mother gives me a quick look. "Mason, are you really concerned about your intelligence?"

"Yes, Mama, I really am." She stares straight out the windshield and I can see her mind grinding out what is really happening to me. Despite all the caution that Charles has advocated, I'm glad that I can be honest with her. Honesty is a concept that I've had trouble with; it's only since I have developed a small ability to lie and deceive that I am able to understand it. I make a promise to myself that I will never attempt to lie to or deceive her.

"This is really remarkable..." she says softly to herself.

I continue my trajectory honestly, albeit relentlessly. "It's not fair that some of us have laptops and others don't. Could you arrange through your grant to Dr. Malone to give laptops to the people in the study who don't have them?" I say, cutting to the chase.

"The grant! You know about the grant?" She looks at me with her eyes wide and her mouth open.

"Yes, I read about it on the Department of Education website."

"You can read and understand that website?" she asks, shaking her head as if trying to clarify her thoughts.

"Yes, with the swinging phonics monkey, the Oxford, and your most-frequent word cards." I explain it all to her, although I don't tell her about the open-doors part in my progress. I think it might be too disconcerting—honest, but not always forthcoming.

We're in the parking lot outside the giant white building that says Education on a small sign next to its entrance, too small a sign for such a large building. We walk into a large room I now know as a lobby; we scurry by a large desk with a sign that says information, behind which two persons in blue uniforms sit, and go through a gate with the two police-people (people, since one is a woman). It takes a long time to go through the multiple checkpoints, elevators, and hallways. Countless long hallways with doors on each side, some open, some closed, that remind me of my hallway full of doors. One long hallway leads to my mother's office. There are two rooms to it, and the furniture is comfortable and well used. I try the couches and chairs—there seem to be too many tables, each sporting a number of books, many of them open, and manuscripts set out in a seemingly random order. The drapes and carpet are dark, look old, and show a lot of wear. The overall effect is warm and somewhat shabby. This is the first time I have been here; she introduces me to various people, and I use my maturing social skills in the process, saying things like "so nice to meet you" and "my name is Mason, I'm thirteen years old." I smile and shake a lot of hands. My mother seems pleased.

"Now I must do those things I came for. You sit here, and I won't be long," she says, and she closes the door to her office, and I sit in the little room outside. After what seems to be a long time, probably only a half-hour or so, I am asked to come in. I still don't have a good grip on time other than the days indicated by the doors. At this point, I measure time only as gaps between events and don't measure time in increments. I tell myself to ask for a watch.

"Now, I can act on your earlier request," she says, as she dials the phone on her desk.

"Hello," I hear Dr. Malone answer. This phone allows me to hear both sides of the conversation.

"Dr. Malone, Marilyn Free here."

"Assistant Secretary," he responds and waits expectantly.

"I hope you're still not angry with me over the social group," she begins.

"Oh, certainly not, everything is fine," he answers with a voice that says he's not telling the truth. Lying through his fucking teeth, Logan would have said. I smile at the thought.

"Well, doctor, the reason I'm calling is I want to ensure all the participants in the study have access to laptops to support their progress."

"Impossible" is his one-word response.

"And why is that, doctor?" she says evenly.

"The design of the study has already been written. A change in the design would invalidate the results. The study would not be able to attribute the changes to the design treatments, but perhaps to the laptops. It's out of the question."

"Well, doctor, the person who called this to my attention tells me that many of the participants already have access to laptop use."

"Who was that?" he asks quickly.

"The person wishes to remain anonymous." She smiles at me and continues. "I'm not a research professional, but it seems you already have that variable operative in your study, and providing everyone with equal access would strengthen the design, not weaken it."

"As you say, you are not a design professional," Dr. Malone states, obviously irritated. He says this flatly as if this ends the interaction.

"What I am, Dr. Malone," continues my mother calmly, "is the federal oversight of your study, design and all." I'm getting a good lesson of what power is. "I am going to give a laptop to every one of the participants who lack one, and I will expect your staff to provide instruction in their use."

There is long silence on the phone, during which Dr. Malone reviews his understanding of power. Then says, "At least give each participant the same laptop. That will help the consistency of the design."

"Will do, doctor," says my mother cheerfully.

12

The Risk of Trust

After the laptop war with Dr. Malone, my mother is uncharacteristically quiet. I find her looking at me throughout the day. Outside of school, I'm mainly working on my computer and watching television. School has recently transformed from a classic waste of time to a fascinating opportunity to observe my fellow Mongoloid students. This gives me an increasing degree of compassion for those with my condition, and also a new respect for Dr. Malone's bazooka and machine gun treatment of Bad Mr. 21. In addition to an augmented compassion, my observations provide instruction on how to act as a traditional Mongoloid. I don't yet know about political correctness, but I intentionally violate it in thought and word. I start to write these principles down; they will become a small pamphlet that will help structure the behavior of the study participants as we try to keep the magnitude of our progress a secret.

Two days after the laptop war, I'm due to return to my father's house. We're eating breakfast in the kitchen and my mother breaks her silence. "What does your father think of your incredible growth?" she asks me hesitantly.

"He doesn't really know. He's helping me learn to read and has been happy about my progress, but I think it makes him nervous—he doesn't have any idea of the extent. But now, I think, he's beginning to understand the study is a good thing."

"Why doesn't he know?"

"Because I've kept it a secret," I answer honestly.

"Why, for heaven's sake?"

"We feel that if people know how well the gene therapy works, they won't think it's a good thing, won't allow us to continue with it. We don't think that they can handle, think it's disorienting." I use a new word in my burgeoning vocabulary.

"We?"

"Me, and the other participants in the study," I answer honestly, realizing that I am jeopardizing the others.

"You've talked this over?" she whispers, barely audible.

"Yes, at the social group."

"That's why you wanted a meeting just between yourselves?" says my mother, catching on.

"Yes." There is a prolonged silence in which she just stares at me. "Mama, I'm violating our rules by telling you all this. You have to keep it secret."

She stands up straight, gazes off into the distance of the kitchen cupboards, and says, "Thank you, Mason, for your trust."

13

The Laptop Hero

At home in my father's house, I'm missing my laptop, but I have access to the to the Oxford through my tablet. I use the dictionary as I watch television news shows, increasing my fluency with words and concepts. At first, concepts come far slower than words, things like democracy and innocent until proven guilty, but as I continue, they become more closely linked. I've stopped asking my father to explain various topics because it seems to trouble him. I remember my awkward foray into government. Disorienting is a useful word, better I think than nervous. My learning with the tablet is less focused and precise than it is with the laptop at my mom's. The tablet is less powerful, but it has a certain benefit. When used along with the television, I am forced to focus on concepts that are useful in understanding society. Society is a notion of which I am just beginning to become aware. Also, hearing the way people talk to each other is useful. By the end of three days at my father's house, I can understand more of what the people on the news are saying and am becoming distressed over a number of the stories.

My mother picks me up on Friday and takes me to the study; playgroup seems a little infantile. At the study, we go to our starting circle. Tangent to the circle of chairs are two stacks of rectangular boxes, each stack about a meter and a half high. Sally is in charge today and tells us that they have determined that some of us have laptops, while others don't, and Dr. Malone has corrected this inequality by arranging to provide everyone with a laptop and the instruction in its use. "Here's to you, Dr. Malone," I think to myself, smiling.

The rest of the playgroup time (why not use the term?) is used to teach us how to operate our new machines. We meet in groups of three, and I'm irritated that Holly is not in my group. The young teachers are in charge and teach some things that I didn't know. We are told to use only this laptop and not others, if we have them, and to bring our new laptops to the playgroup each time we come. "Thanks a lot, Dr. Malone, for your progressive thinking." I whisper to myself.

Charles uses the parent pick-up time to tell each participant to bring their laptop to the social group meeting that will take place at his home this evening.

14

The Second Social Group

All of the students are present at this second meeting of our social group. I would later find out that my mother had called each parent to say that attendance, though not specifically required, is strongly encouraged by the study. My trust in her seems not to be misplaced.

The social group takes place in the large living room of Charles's home, situated in a neighborhood of enormous houses, with expanses of lawn that shine in the light rain that falls. There is food and drink set out on tables, and Madonna sings on the CD player. Charles' parents are solicitous, trying to make everyone feel comfortable and included, and show no signs of leaving us alone. Finally, Charles asks them for privacy and they acquiesce. The room is large with enough seats for all of us, with a leather couch capable of seating half our group. There is an iron-and-glass coffee table, two mounted animal heads that gaze down from the wall—one I know is a moose, the other is a deer-like thing with long spiral horns. Holly is appalled and remains uneasy through the duration of the meeting. Some of us sit on pillows on the floor. Holly sits beside me with her back to the animal heads. We arrange ourselves, as we did in the first social group, in an approximate circle incorporating the leather couch. Charles again assumes the leadership of the group. "Well, we need to thank the actions of Dr. Malone for getting all of us laptops, although I'm surprised he did it."

"He didn't," I say, and I give a brief account of how it all came down. Charles looks a little embarrassed.

"Well, then, we are right to distrust him. And I think we should continue our policy." We all nod in agreement. He continues: "I've been doing some research on how we can be in contact with each other between these meetings. Does anyone know about email?" I had read the term on various websites but did not know what it was.

"Fuckin' A," says Logan. "My asshole father uses it with his piece of shit patients, my sister's emails are more fucking interesting, however. It's like sending little letters over the Internet. The little cunt (another word I'll have to define, though Logan's used it before) uses it to talk to her dickhead boyfriend and plan all sorts of shit that my parents don't motherfucking know about." He stops, looking well satisfied.

"As Logan has just told us, email is a way we can use our new laptops to communicate with each other, to share information about the new things we are finding out about. My father's an IT professional. IT means information technology, email, laptops, stuff like that, and I've read a number of books about it. If you don't know about it, you can learn it quickly, it's not that hard, at least for us." Charles smiles. "I think we should all sign up for an email address, and practice using it, before we leave tonight."

Nobody has a better idea, so Charles guides us in acquiring email addresses, and we do this with little trouble. Everyone's skills are progressing in step. Some may have more information than others, but we all seem to have developed similar capabilities. Holly has a bit of trouble that I help her through. I attribute her problems to her unease with the surrounding environment and the severed animal heads. We practice sending each other short messages.

"Now," continues Charles, "there's another issue we must attend to—encryption."

It's a new word for all of us, and even Logan is fucking ignorant. "Encryption," Charles explains, "is like a code that keeps other people from being able to read our messages. It ensures our privacy." He elaborates: "I read a whole book about it my father's library last night; it's becoming a hot topic in IT. I've downloaded an encryption program, used my dad's account to get it, and I can transfer it to us, then we'll all be able to message each other without fear that someone, like Dr. Malone, can violate our privacy."

At this point, Charles's mother comes in to see if we need anything; Charles sends her politely away. "You all see the need for privacy, and the importance of encryption to our emails," he says, smiling, and looks to the place that his mother has just exited.

We acknowledge the need for privacy and encryption. Charles links his computer to each of ours and transfers the program, then using the Internet, he sends us all an email. When we retrieve it, we find an incomprehensible text of numbers and symbols. We look at him and he smiles. "That's what anyone who hacks into our emails will see." Hacking, he explains, is the process of someone trying to violate our privacy by entering our emails. "In order to read the texts as they were written, you will need a password, like you made for your email account earlier. We will need to come up with a password we can all use to de-encrypt each other's messages. Does anyone have an idea for a password that we won't forget?" A few of us laugh, since with our development, forgetting is a concept now only operative in our past. A boy named John suggests *Mongoloid Freedom*.

"Too short," critiques Charles. "We need something a little more complex. Do you wish to expand it?" John remains silent.

The irrepressible Logan again speaks up. "I've been reading about prohibition, you know when they outlawed alcohol." Our group looks at him blankly, but he continues. "If you wanted a motherfucking drink you had to go to a speakeasy, a secret place where alcohol was served. What you'd did is knock three times on the door and ask for douchebag Joe. I think a good password is knock 3 times and ask for Joe."

"Attila," I interject reflexively. The blank stares of the group are now transferred from Logan to me. And I spend some time talking about my research on Mongolian people and the term Mongoloid.

"Knock 3 times and ask for Attila is a great password. No one will break it!" says Charles, and we all agree. "It's good, too, since we need a number in it, along with a capital letter."

John speaks for a second time. "How are we supposed keep our progress secret at the behavioral clinic? What can we show them we know and what can't we?"

It's a good question, and I take a crack at it using my recent experience with my differential behavior with my father and mother. I suggest we should show some progress but conceal the true extent of our abilities, especially the fact that we may be becoming far more intelligent than most people in society. I continue, "If we show some growth and achievement it will demonstrate that the study seems to be working." Then I tell them about my observations of my fellow students, and how I've been writing up rules that if followed would not bring undue scrutiny. I say I'll finish this up and send it to everyone via encrypted email for their review and comments. People nod and agree that it is a reasonable approach.

We're getting to the end of the two-hour social group; I check the new watch that I got my father to buy me, ostensibly so he can teach me how to tell time. It's an underwater watch that I think looks sporty. It's good to 30 meters. I, myself, am only good to 1 meter, but I'm quite proud of it and have flashed it in front of Holly at every opportunity.

"Before we go," says Charles, "I would suggest we do a few things to prepare us for our next social group. The first is that we write down and post what our parents do for their work, along with this state what you are most interested in learning about. My father is an IT guy, so it was easy for me to access information about emails and encryptions. Mason has used his mother to provide us a number of resources, like the laptops and, indeed, the social group itself. Logan used his father's resources to our benefit (motherfucking benefit I amend in my mind). I'm sure you have parents with resources that could prove important to us. After we reach the same levels of general knowledge, identifying our interests is important so we don't end up researching the same things. Then we can report our findings back the whole group."

Our time is almost over, and Charles's mother keeps surreptitiously peeking around the corner. Charles is not unaware of this and says, "In closing, I think we should refer to ourselves collectively as the Attila Group." We all nod, or grunt, our agreement.

I think Charles is a sharp cookie. Fuckin' A.

15

Profiles

What I'm writing is less a history of the Attilian Movement, if I may call it that, than an account of my history within it; as such, my descriptions can tend to be narrow and incomplete. A chief area of these omissions is in the backstories of the individuals involved. To address this deficiency, I am including profiles of some of the major characters important to the progression of my narrative. The profiles consist of information gathered by me through my interactions and by material I've asked the individuals to provide me in writing, so what appears here is a hopefully not-too-amateurish mixture of a first- and second-person account of the individual being profiled. I add these at certain points in the narrative where the individual becomes prominent. By this, it is my intention to flesh out a more expansive view of our story.

Profile: Charles

Charles, at the time of writing is fifteen, one of the older members of the group and initially one of the most astute. He tends to be skeptical and questioning in his approach to life, its situations, and his place in it. This, I feel, is less a part of his basic nature than it is the result of the analysis he puts into addressing the questions and situations he is concerned with. However, his critical view does not extend to his friendships and social interactions; in these, he is warm and accepting.

His family is made up of his father, his mother, and two older brothers about a year and a half apart. Charles came along later in the lives of his parents and is five years younger than his youngest brother. Maternal age might have been a factor in his Mongolism; his mother was 44 at the time of his birth, this from a school file we obtained via Langdon University (more on that later). His father is an outdoorsman, as are his brothers. The family spends time hiking, camping, kayaking, and canoeing on the Chesapeake, and on hunting trips around the United States, and even once to Africa. When Charles was born, he was welcomed into the tight family and included into all its activities, including the outdoor ones.

He writes:

> *My first vivid memory was when my family went kayaking on the Chesapeake river. I must have been about three or four; my father and two brothers had solo kayaks, two red ones and a blue one. But my mother had a two-man kayak and it was bright yellow. I remember that yellow color stood out from the surrounding water in a way that my father's and brothers' didn't. My mother strapped me into the floatation vest attending to it carefully. "If you fall overboard just don't worry it will keep above water." I thought at the time if I fell out of the kayak I would float suspended in the air over the water, and the thought was pleasant. Anyway, after checking and rechecking my vest she put me in the front hole of the boat and handed me a little paddle, not a kayak paddle but one you'd use in a canoe.*
>
> *She pushed the kayak about halfway out into the river, simultaneously entering the rear hole. She employed her two-bladed paddle and we were off, carried gently along by the current where I could feel myself rocking. I could see the*

two blades of her paddle as they reached out beside me, then alternatively dove into the water and pushed us forward. I was overcome by the beauty and freedom that surrounded me on the water of that river. Although I didn't have words for it, the feeling has lasted.

I dipped my paddle into the river wanting to help as the sun glinted on the disturbed water and ran way in little concentric circles growing ever bigger. I was infatuated.

Phase II

Progress

16

Rules for Being Mongoloid

As I promised, at the second social group, I've put together a small pamphlet on how to deploy ourselves as traditional Mongoloids and keep the degree of our group's ever-increasing abilities secret. The principles are derived from the observations I made at my school of my fellow students. I'm in an Integrated School, which means a school for typical students where students with disabilities are placed, with various supports, into regular classrooms with typical students. Hereafter, I will use the term "Typical" throughout this work as a synonym for non-handicapped people. The word is finding prominence in scientific and professional journals dealing with the subject of disability. Its use implies no inherent superiority. However, I use it deliberately to emphasize a social distinction. I capitalize it as I do "Mongoloid" to indicate the tribal nature of the groups. At various times, we retards meet in homogenous groups composed of only people with disabilities—the higher we go in school, and the more advanced the curriculum becomes, the more prevalent these groupings.

The educational demand on me is minimal, so I have unimpeded time to observe, and in some cases, employ certain experiments. These observations are supported by readings in the medical and educational literature on Down Syndrome.

I'm becoming more fluent in the mores of society, and I've come to realize that my use of words could be termed politically incorrect or viewed as insensitive. From the beginning, I've favored words like Mongoloids, retards, tards (a word in its own right used to infuse an extra degree of derision by its use), feebs, morons, imbeciles, and mental defectives to describe our conditions. I first used them sensing their innate power. I continue to use them since it calls attention to the pigeon holes, or boxes, society places us in. I use them to foster mindfulness in the Attila group that our environment is not entirely friendly or benign.

My observations, readings, and research, as it is presented in the pamphlet, focus on rules of how we should operate to minimize the extent to which we are becoming a bit of a new species in a somewhat hostile land.

How to Operate with Issues Independent of Intelligence

> • *Mongoloids are defined through their passivity. People expect us to be friendly and accepting in most interactions with Typicals. Try not to be frustrated, even when Typicals are obviously wrong or stupid in their behavior or requests. If a request is patently unreasonable, just don't react. Mongoloids are often thought to be stubborn.*
>
> • *Mongoloids don't generally demonstrate a strong focus when approaching a task, so do not use a strong penetrating gaze and slightly protrude your tongue and act a bit distracted. It is, however, OK to stare directly at someone and smile. While eye contact is not to be avoided, do not stare or use a penetrating gaze.*
>
> • *Mongoloids are not demanding. Don't insist on your wants; try to go through a back door. Typicals are not that discerning, so misdirection is often easy. Under no circumstances be contentious or insistent even when you are correct or have a better way to do something.*

> • *Mongoloids are thought to be loving and affectionate. In an uncomfortable, or awkward, situation, employ a hug, say "I love you," while gaining control of yourself.*
>
> • *Mongoloids are thought to be mostly happy. Try not to show a sad emotion.*
>
> • *Mongoloids demonstrate concern for others, particularly with respect to how people in their environment are feeling; once again, go to hugs and "I love yous."*

These principles represent ways we can distract Typicals from identifying our newly acquired knowledge and abilities. Practice using them under safe conditions.

How to Operate with Issues of Intelligence

• *While behavioral and physical deployment are important, it is Intelligence that is the central issue of being Mongoloid. The fact that we are mentally retarded has defined our status from the beginning. As with other disabilities, mental retardation has garnered sympathy but more often derision. Terms like: retard, tard, moron, imbecile, idiot, feeb (a shortened form of feeble-minded), mental defective, and indeed, Mongoloid itself are applied to us both individually and collectively as a group. These are also applied as putdowns to Typicals, or to describe inept or substandard behavior. These terms are used generally as a synonym for stupidity. Try not to demonstrate acts that bring attention to your intelligence, particularly when it surpasses an action of a Typical.*

• *Mongoloids are defined by their inability to learn. Retarded is a word that signifies the slowing of progress or skills acquisition. However, in our case, the slowing is viewed as a permanent condition. With that general expectation, try not to acquire new skills too quickly or too proficiently, as this can be anticipated to cause disorientation, if not inadvertent hostility. With noticeable radical strides in our learning and intelligence, we can anticipate those involved to be at the least puzzled and disoriented. Hilda's interaction with her mother around bathwater is just one example.*

17

Applying and Ignoring the Rules

My record on applying these rules to myself, along with my fidelity to them, is certainly a mixed bag. At home with my father, I mostly employ them with a few exceptions directed toward his education. However gentle, these are often disturbing, and I kept them to a minimum. At the play group, aware that I'm under scrutiny, I am careful to observe them impeccably, though I'm aware of an increasing skepticism on the part of Dr. Malone. The play group is tricky since I'm obliged to show some growth that supports the study while not giving away the extent of its success.

With my mother, however, I have mostly abandoned them; it is here that I'm free to live honestly in my emerging self. This is both invigorating and a bit dangerous as it increasingly relaxes my vigilance. As my confidence increases, it seeps into my other life roles and I often find that, like a stage actor who has failed to change his costume between scenes, I am awkward and exposed.

It was becoming exponentially more difficult to live with a foot in two camps and clear I would have to exercise more caution and awareness of my differing environments. As it turned out, I proved unable to animate that caution when I embarked on an ill-conceived research project of my own. It would result in unfortunate consequences.

18

Calculus

The school I attend, Georgetown Middle School, is primarily for upper-middle-class Typicals. It's a progressive school, and, as I've explained previously, persons with disabilities are integrated into various classes and school activities; as classes progress in difficulty, there is less integration, and it is restricted to offerings such as art, music, P.E., and the big one—lunch. Even shop and cooking classes are restricted since we are thought to be at risk around tools and stoves.

I embark on a little first-hand research on the dangers of exposing one's new abilities to Typicals. My research begins with cooking class. Over the extent of the special cooking class, I had been impeccable in all of my activities, demonstrating mastery of concepts and equipment, so I asked to be allowed to enroll in the Typical cooking class. The teacher even supported my request, which went to the top administration, where it was dismissed as not safe. All my appeals were summarily denied. None of the supporting arguments or data, such as a letter submitted by the cooking teacher, were considered, probably not even read. I was not discouraged as this supported my observations and hypothesis. I then decided to up the ante. It required a little risk, but I decided what the hell. Advanced Placement or A.P. courses were becoming common for the more capable students. If a student successfully passed an A.P. course she or he could receive college credit. There were many of these courses offered by our school, and I picked one to infiltrate.

After my experience with cooking, I thought it prudent to begin with my school counselor, whom I share with Typicals, and ask to be enrolled in the intermediate calculus class. Mr. Brandsma, the counselor, looks shocked that I can even say intermediate calculus, much less qualify for it—but my mother carries considerable weight, and Mr. Brandsma is cautious to treat me with *faux* respect and courtesy.

"Well, you know, Mason, you need other math classes before you take this one," he says, condescension moistening his smiling lips.

Here, he expects me to leave the office along with my absurd, if arcane, request. "They say you can take a test," I say without eye contact, my mouth open, and my tongue slightly protruding.

"Well, yes, but no one has ever entered that class by a test," he says, becoming irritated.

"I want to try," I say, violating my rule against non-insistence and confrontation." He looks at me as if his desk lamp has just spoken.

"Well, I don't schedule the tests or grant approval to A.P. courses, that's done by Mr. Meanan." Mr. Meanan is the vice principal. I know him from my failed cooking course rebellion; I'm sure he'll be happy to hear from me again. I smile around my protruding tongue.

"Let's go and speak to him," I say, further violating my insistence principle. I believe my mother again tips the scale.

"Well," he says, not making a move to leave.

"Well, let's go," I say, again violating any number of my principles.

We traverse the 10 meters to the vice principal's office. Mr. Brandsma sounds embarrassed as he asks the secretary if we can be seen. The vice principal is meeting with a student, but we are told he will be done soon. We sit along the wall with other miscreants awaiting an audience.

A penitent student soon exits, and the secretary tells us to go in. Mr. Meanan looks at me as if someone has set a skunk free in his office. He continues to look silently at the odorous mammal. "Tell him your request," states the courageous counselor.

"I want to take the test to enroll in intermediate calculus," the desk lamp speaks.

His initial reaction is a reflexive laugh, then remembering who my mother is, and the cooking skirmish, he gains control of himself. "Mason, what makes you think that you are ready for such an advanced class?" Not waiting for me to respond, he continues, "I even haven't had that class."

I'm not surprised, I think, as I respond to his question. "I've been studying arithmetic on my own, and I'd like to take the test." I use the term arithmetic rather than math to further ratchet down expectations and put him off his guard. I had been studying math on my own, as I studied everything else, and I was currently working through linear algebra and quantum mechanics.

"Arithmetic…" he mouths. He's quiet for a moment while coming to a decision, "OK, Mason, I'll give Mr. Brandsma the test. Can he take it in your office tomorrow, Jerry?"

"Absolutely, Ken, I'll make arrangements with his teachers."

"It's quite an extensive test and may take you a good deal of time," Meanan says as he smiles at Jerry. "Good luck, boy." I had just read *The Catcher in the Rye*, where Holden Caulfield comments that "Good Luck" is a terrible thing to say, if you really think about it. I know how he felt.

It was indeed an extensive test and not real user-friendly. I wasn't surprised that no one had ever entered the calculus course by the test. Even if you were familiar with the concepts, there were a number of devious misdirections. I navigated through the test and its potholes in two hours sitting at a table set up in the counselor's waiting room, while other students came and went with their concerns.

Brandsma has a key to the test answers and brings me into his office while he scores my responses. He says nothing but shows increasing agitation as he continues. When he finishes, he looks at me with a puzzled expression. He continues his silence, stands up, and gestures me to follow.

In Meanan's office, the vice principal's solicitous smile changes quickly to incomprehension, then to anger. "Who put you up to this?" he says.

"Nobody," I say looking down at the floor. "Do you want me to take it again?"

Meanan is not paying any attention, staring off into the horizon of his bookcase. "How is this possible?" he asks Jerry. "Was there anyone else in the room when he took this test?" He hits the test he is holding with his other hand.

Brandsma is hesitant with his response. "There were a variety of students who came and went throughout the testing period, but no one who was there the entire time."

"Who were they?" Meanan demands, and Brandsma lists a number of students who were present. "None of these students know anything about higher math," he spits out. Then to me, he says, "This is some kind of trick." Then, primarily to himself, "Nobody gets a perfect score."

The statement requires no response, so I remain quiet, with tongue protruding and an unfocused gaze.

"Tell me who put you up to this? How did you do it?" he asks.

"Nobody," I say again. "I study math on my own. You can review the worksheets I produced to get the answers. Can I take the class now?"

"Over my dead body," he screams, "I'm going to get to the bottom of this." I confess that I am taking a perverse delight in all of this on the part of demeaned Mongoloids throughout history. My anger hypothesis is strengthened when Meanan grabs me by the lapels of my shirt and Brandsma quickly interjects.

"Ken, his mother." This seems to have a somewhat sobering effect on the vice principal, who orders us out of his office with the promise to continue this matter later.

My elation causes me to push it, "Can I take the course now?"

"No!" He hollers as Mr. Brandsma shepherds me into the relative safety of the waiting room.

19

Mental Retardation Defined

I have made a study of mental retardation and intelligence, and from that study have come up with what I believe is an original and functional definition of mental retardation: *Mental retardation is a deficiency in generalization and discrimination*. Generalization is the facility that allows one to distinguish how different things are similar. Discrimination is the facility to distinguish how similar things are different. People who are deemed intelligent can both generalize and discriminate at high levels, and as such, manipulate the environment to their advantage. People with mental retardation demonstrate these abilities at lower levels and, as such, are often vulnerable to their environment.

I build on my definition of mental retardation with a definition of intelligence. *Intelligence is the accumulation of both knowledge and skills.* Knowledge is knowing about things, while skills concern knowing how to do specific things. Intelligent people know a lot about a variety of things—both general and specific, and have the skills to do specific procedures valued by society. Tards don't know a lot of either. These simple definitions are all that is needed to understand mental retardation and intelligence. Working from these principles, I further expand and elaborate the rules.

> • *Mongoloids are not supposed to learn very well or (get very far with their learning). It is important that our learning should be demonstrated in small steps and used only to increase our independence so that we can function more on our own.*

My research project with Brandsma and Meanan established, as far as I was concerned, the validity of the danger of demonstrating the magnitude of our learning ability. I go on with the rules.

> • *Don't demonstrate your knowledge to others, as it will call attention to your emerging intelligence. As a general rule, keep your knowledge from Typicals; only let it out in little bits and then only to foster confidence in your independence.*
>
> • *Skills demonstrate our ability to do things. As a rule, only demonstrate skill for simple things, like your ability to cross the street safely, take the right bus, and to not put inedible objects in your mouth (unless it's a bassoon which, of course, is unlikely). When Logan fixed his father's stereo, he "fucked up," by placing himself in a superior position to a Typical. It was probably benign since his father would be forgiving, but avoid doing that with Typicals in society. They will at best resent you, and at worst feel threatened.*
>
> • *Generalization and discrimination are about making connections from two different, but linked, vantage points. Don't demonstrate your facility with making connections; the more astute the connection, the more exposed we make ourselves.*
>
> • *Realize that while Mongoloids don't do well with generalization, discrimination, knowledge, and skills, neither do Typicals. They do better than tards, but only just*

barely, and in some cases not at all. Facility with any of these will call undue attention to us, by making the thin line between Mongoloids and Typicals thinner. This is to be avoided until we have time to map out our future destiny.

With this, the brief pamphlet ends and becomes the subject of much discussion within the Attila Group.

20

More Calculus

Back to calculus. I'm picked up late at school by my mother. As I get into the car she says, "I got a call from Mr. Meanan as I was leaving the office." After a short pause, she presses on. "Do you want to tell me what it's about?"

"No," I say honestly.

"Well, baby, why don't you try."

"It's about calculus," I mumble, barely audible.

"Yes, calculus that's what Mr. Meanan tried to explain. Do you even know what calculus is?"

"Yes, it's a mathematical way to partition reality into smaller units in order to solve certain problems."

"Partition reality? Mason, what's happening?" My mother has pulled off the road and is now looking straight at me. She's serious but not totally shocked, so I know she's beginning to understand the situation on her own.

"It's about Bad Mr. 21," I begin, and I go on to tell her everything, including my efforts to protect the Attila Group and my experiment first with cooking and now calculus. I tell her about my recent efforts to learn mathematics.

"Mason, this is wonderful."

"It's not all wonderful, Mama. You can see that by the reaction of Mr. Meanan. He doesn't see it as wonderful. It only makes him angry."

"He's angry because he thinks you cheated and someone is playing a joke on him."

"No, Mama, he's angry because his worldview has been challenged, and it makes him uncomfortable—people don't like to feel uncomfortable. Other people in our group have experienced similar examples. My research is simply a controlled experiment that I designed in order to establish a fact."

"Mason, you talk like a scientist," my mother whispers.

My cover already blown, I say, "I'm beyond that, Mama." I continue: "You have to promise me you'll keep our secret. You're the only Typical to know about us. We need time to gain our bearings." She seems to consider this for a little while, and I'm getting nervous.

"I'll keep your secret, Mason," she says at last. "But you will have to promise me back to keep me informed of your progress." She waits for my response.

"I will," I say, and mean it.

"Typicals," she whispers to herself.

The next day, we both go into the school to meet with the vice principal. Mr. Meanan has calmed down considerably, but he's still adamant that I was involved in a practical joke, not that I was bright enough to have planned it on my own.

My mother has her consummate professional's hat on and is extremely courteous and polite but holds Vice principal Meanan's feet to the fire with respect to any evidence that I had not taken the test in good faith. Meanan maintains that it is obvious. I am a Mongoloid, and that's that. He doesn't need evidence. My mother remains calm and establishes that there is a second form of the test and suggests that I take it in Meanan's office with him acting as the proctor. I try to call off this game of chicken. I've already proved what I set out to. But my mother is unmoved, and Meanan takes my protestation as an admission of guilt, so the test is immediately set up. My mother stays at school and asks for a tour that makes everyone nervous for the next two hours.

Brandsma is summoned to score the new test and looks uncomfortable under our gaze. The result is the same. The vice-principal is livid and demonstrates his conviction by risking the anger and possible retribution of my mother, whose professional hat is quickly slipping. At this point, I say I don't want to go to the class anymore. And refuse to change my mind. The vice-principal again takes this as an admission of some kind of chicanery, but for me to continue with it would bring further unwanted attention and scrutiny. I have found out what I had set out to and further demonstrated to my mother our need for secrecy. We leave Meanan puzzling over my written worksheets that might as well have been written in Greek.

21

Selling Short

We are now two months into the Bad Mr. 21 gene therapy. Between that and the laptops, most of us have achieved a general education superior to most PhDs, although we have succeeded in disguising the bulk of our learning, yet the gene therapy program is thought to be a raging success. I'd located an interim report Dr. Malone had submitted to the journal *Human Genetics* where he preened in the initial results of his study. While I still didn't trust him, and disliked his pomposity, I had to acknowledge a monumental debt to his bazooka and machine gun therapy. We all did.

To read Dr. Malone's communication I'd have to subscribe to the journal, which costs money. So, I use a trial subscription to receive a one-time read, but to read more I'd have to pay. I didn't have access to any money, so I call Charles, who had used his father's credit card to fund the encryption program. I am told by him that it was tricky since his father monitors his account scrupulously. "I had a hell of a time trying to explain the encryption expense, and in the end, I don't think he believed me anyway."

I knew I could have asked my mother and she would have provided the funds for a subscription; she probably had a copy of the article. But I preferred not to involve her in the more subversive aspects of our progress. I realized that keeping our secret was taking a certain toll on her. If I asked my father, he'd have a heart attack.

The next social group is at Logan's, and we meet in his father's study with the infamous stereo. I tell the group about Dr. Malone's article and how it would be enlightening to read. "I can get it for us with my butthead father's Visa card. I've used it a lot, my father's clueless." Logan pulls out his laptop, makes some entries, looks up and smiles. "Done," he says. "To access it sign in with my email address and use the password Speakeasy."

While we each have been on our individual educational odysseys, there has been little coordination between group members. As a result, most of us tend to follow the careers and expertise of our parents. Charles investigated his father's IT library and guided our laptop use, making sure our correspondence was encrypted. Amy's parents are both chemists, her father quite famous. So, she used her time to learn chemistry. I followed my mother's sojourn into governmental power.

I suggest creating some working groups to focus on specific topics: The first is our genetic condition and ongoing therapy, the second is a more recent realization and concerns ways to make money to fund our group's activities.

Andrew, a skinny and tentative older boy, raises his hand to be acknowledged. He stutters slightly and had spoken before the group only a few times. "Ha-have any of you heard of the Stock Ma Market?" he begins haltingly. I had run across the term in my reading of the *Washington Post* and knew it was important part of the economy but knew little else.

"Wa-well, the most important businesses are funded through the selling of shares, little bits of ownership in that company. When the company increases in value, the value of the shares also increases. When you sell the shares back, you make the difference between how much you paid and how much you sold it for. Like it's ca-complicated, but I think the stock market might be a way to create funds for us." Andrew then tells us that his father manages a hedge fund, and he's been teaching him about buying stock, and that he even has a personal trading account and, so far, has made $20,000. We all decide that this is worth pursuing and vow to research it on our own.

While no working groups are formed before we disband, everyone agrees to read *Human Genetics* and research the stock market.

After the social group, there is a flurry of communication between us about the stock market as we attempt to gain mastery of the medium. We all set up faux accounts and try our hand with a variety of success, but collectively we make $2,000 in five days. I message Mary, whose father is a lawyer; Charles, whose father is the IT guy; and Andrew, whose father is the hedge fund wizard, and we work together to create a collective account, so we can begin to use real money.

By the next social group, we are set; Charles takes the lead. "Andrew, Mary, and I have worked together to establish a joint trading account where we can all participate in the stock market. Andrew, who already has an active account, transferred $15,000 to get us started, so we can make real-life trades, or real-life losses. We all made money last week with our pretend accounts—nice work, everyone. We should get better as we gain familiarity with the system. Does anyone have anything they would like to report? Yes, Logan."

"Last week I learned the system and made just a little. The son-of-a-bitch'n system requires that you predict the positive trends in the stocks you buy, so that you can sell higher than you bought. The shit of it is, Typicals are really dumb, and it's hard to anticipate how the assholes think—they're just not rational. So, I was thinking that there should be some way I could bet on the dumbfuck moves the market would make, and I found a technique called selling short. You guys will need to learn about it because it's a little more complicated, but you fucking bet on a stock going down, which is easier since I've found that Typicals have far more dumb ideas than they do good ones. Essentially, you buy bets on what a stock will do in the future, these bets are called puts, and are traded like stocks. Like I said, it's a little fuckin' complicated, and takes a little more time, but it's way the shit better than relying on stocks to increase. I'm way ahead on all the puts I've bought."

No one knew anything about selling short, not even Charles and Andrew, but we were intrigued. We formed a selling-short working group, with eight of us agreeing to research this and share the findings with each other— added to Charles, Mary, and Andrew's, it is our first real working group. The rest agreed to continue with the positive side of the stock market. Charles brought us back to the present, saying, "Thanks to Andrew, we now have some real money to experiment with and a place to park our gains. Fifteen thousand isn't a lot spread between 15 people. But at least we can each have $1,000 to play with over the next week." We all left the social group with not a word said about gene therapy, but with a new feeling of collective purpose that didn't have anything to do with being Mongoloids in transition.

Profile: Andrew

Andrew's father was a genius, even by Mongoloid standards. He was a hedge fund wizard, which meant he used high-risk means, such as borrowed funds and high-risk buys, to engage the stock market and amass large profits quickly. It's risky, with no guarantees, but the returns could be immense, and Andrew's father was a master, anticipating trends that were often counterintuitive, or out of left field (as my father might say), by exercising a keen but radically different eye. It was this radically divergent eye that saw things the way they should be and allowed them to come true. This was exactly the approach he used with his son, refusing to acknowledge his limitations.

Andrew writes:

> "My father always saw things the way he wanted, it was true for his business, it was true for me. When I began to exhibit the changes brought on by the demise of Bad Mr. 21, my father didn't even notice, or notice much. Our relationship changed not a bit. He involved me in the hedge fund business from my time as a toddler. Always consulting me on his proposed moves, even before I could talk. I was a tentative kid, perhaps because my mother abandoned us soon after I was born, taking an early payoff from the divorce— Dad got off cheaply. It's always been just the two of us.
>
> "He tells a story that when I was young, I often walked with my hands in my front pockets. A friend of his said that this showed I would be a rich man, invoking the character of Quintin from Faulkner's The Sound and the Fury. Later reading the novel, I found Quintin not a very sympathetic

character. Despite this, my father always called me Quintin, whenever we were accessing the stock market."

As Andrew grew into the effects of gene replacement, he showed an acumen similar to his father's, and all Attilians benefited. I was taken by his account of *The Sound and the Fury*, particularly because as a major literary work, the book begins in the mind of an idiot.

22

Charley

During the last month of the study, we are consumed with finding out everything we can concerning gene therapy and the exact nature of the bazooka blasts. Amy, our budding chemist, takes the lead on the investigation. She relates that the injection turns off most of the extra genes of the third chromosome 21—that's actually chromosome 22. This is the initial intent of the injection, but in addition to turning off the effects caused by the extra genes, the injection has had the unanticipated benefit of turning on additional functions of some genes on the extra third chromosome that interact with our regular genes, contributing to our incredible learning capacity.

Amy informs us that the ability of one gene to influence two or more biological factors is called "Pleiotropy." This pleiotropy, along with the turning off of the other extra genes, seems to orchestrate the effects we are experiencing.

Andrea, a member of the group, relates seeing an old movie called

Charley, where a retarded individual is given an injection that increases his intelligence to high Typical levels, but the changes prove not to be permanent. She asks Amy how we know that this will not be the case with us. Amy answers confidently that she too has seen the movie, but it is a work of fiction, and cells of our body changed by the injections are reproduced along with those changes as new cells are produced. Our subscription to the journal *Human Genetics* continues to provide us with information about the Bad Mr. 21 study.

"Besides," Amy says, "we've already duplicated the chemical in my father's lab. So, we have access to it if we should ever need it." Amy periodically has entry to her father's lab in a wing of their house. She has also developed a cadre of group members who are her fellow investigators. In our future, this group will become very important to us.

Our group is increasingly aware of the mechanics that have led to our dramatic increase in intellectual level and capacity; Amy's understanding and facility as a research biochemist is, I would estimate, at the level of an advanced postdoc. Our collective understanding of the biology of genetics is now at the level of a professional with a master's degree and growing. It is becoming increasingly more difficult to keep our gains under wraps.

Profile: Amy

Amy was born to illustrious parents who were both chemists. Her father was a famous physical chemist nominated twice for a Nobel Prize. He treated his failure to win with an equanimity he was almost as renowned for as his science. Amy's birth caused him little concern, as did the accompanying diagnosis of low intelligence, since he was confident that he was smarter than almost everybody else on the planet anyway, and he slipped into the role of Amy's father as seamlessly as he had for his other two children. Amy's mother was a biochemist of note who had, as a young woman, done work on the synthesizing of estrogen, missing the boat by a number of decades, to a German chemist who was first to synthesize it, garnering the Nobel. Still, her estrogen research and her subsequent work had earned her a prestigious place in the chemistry world. Her take on Amy's entry into the family was a bit different than her husband's balanced approach, feeling guilt from her advanced age. And Amy, since her arrival, was always the preferred child of her mother, granting her access to the extensive home laboratory, where Amy crawled over the sterile floors, pulling herself up using her mother's stool to observe the various experiments and apparatuses bubbling on the long counter. The laboratory was off-limits to the other children, but for Amy, it was her playpen.

Toddler Amy would sit on the floor and listened closely to her parents' esoteric exchanges, head moving from one speaker to the next, that on one occasion prompted her father to ask seriously, "You don't think she can understand us, do you?" Amy's mother looked down at her daughter sitting cross-legged on the floor with her slack mouth slightly open, smiled, and said, "I really don't think so, but then again, who can tell?" Amy remembered these conversations from her version of "door openings."

She writes:

> *My most vivid memory of the lab are the smells; I would stick out my tongue and try to taste them. Once when my mother was not looking I tasted the chemical whose pungent sweet smell I liked the best. It was in a small beaker the size of a shot glass. One time my family was on a vacation traveling across Arizona to the Grand Canyon; we were going through the extensive stretch of sand dunes, they looked to me like a tan ocean. The sun was going down and the sand glowed an orange-brown. I begged my parents to let me run through it, so they pulled over to the side of the road and I got out and galloped across the billowy scallops. At one point I jumped as high into the air as I could, folded my legs under me, and fell anticipating a soft landing. It was like landing on concrete, my breath fled from my chest, my teeth clacked together, my spine shimmied and my neck cracked. I was so surprised that I didn't cry, just sat there on the sand gasping for breath. I was so embarrassed and ashamed of my stupidity that I stood up and did a little dance to show that everything was fine. When I sipped the chemical that day in the lab, it was again like landing on concrete. My throat burned, my eyes watered, I gagged and coughed, but was too embarrassed to let anyone, much less my mother, know*

what I had done—it was just like the sand dunes. When I got a hold of myself, my mother who was still unaware and working at her bench, I brought the little beaker over to her and asked her in my limited vocabulary what it was.

"Benzene," she replied.

"Why?" I said, using my favorite word. My mother knew I was not asking why it was benzene, but that I was asking for more information.

"I use it as a non-polar solvent," she answered me straightforwardly, and returned to the activities in front of her.

I tried unsuccessfully to reproduce the word solvent, but my mother turned around, picked me up, hugged me, and said, "That's wonderful, Amy." Starting off with such a bonehead action of sipping benzene, this praise made it worth it. Benzene, it turned out, is a major carcinogen, and chemists now substitute a variety of non-polar solvents, but it smelled like heaven to me.

After the start of the gene therapy program, my father was first to notice the subtle changes I was demonstrating. He brought this to the attention of my mother, who was interested but skeptical. When they became aware that I was beginning to read, they both went apeshit and showered me with opportunities for learning. They put so much energy into me that my sisters began to exhibit jealousy—my mother quickly jumped in to remedy the situation and family harmony was restored.

Amy did not try to hide her progress, but rather engaged her parents as partners, much like I did with my mother. She continues:

When I had progressed to a level where I could engage in mutual conversation, I asked my father what it was that had alerted him to my immerging intellect; he said that it was the nature of the questions I asked.

"It was your curiosity to understand the world that most

engaged me," he said, "I couldn't help but think that you reminded me of myself as a young man trying to solve the world's mysteries."

Both my parents were schooled in evolutionary biology, incorporating its perspective and logic into their work. This seemed to make sense to me, and I set out to learn all I could about it. My mother was the one to employ it most often, looking to evolution and its mechanisms of mutation, adaptation, migration, drift, and selection in her scientific explanations of microbiological phenomena. The evolutionary perspective is the launch point for all of my work. Indeed, the process of gene therapy, suppression, and enhancement, I view as an evolutionary next step in our species.

23

Chemicals, IQ, and Bad Mr. 21's Assassin

Another issue is becoming increasingly important. After thinking I got out of my little research project relatively unscathed, my foray into intermediate calculus again rears its ugly head. Vice principal Meanan refuses to let the incident go and continues to feel he's been duped, and he conducts an investigation, interviewing a number of students, and even some teachers, including the cooking teacher who supported me in my quest to enroll in a Typical cooking class. Rather than getting to the bottom it, the investigation has the effect of advertising the incident. With all the attention, the incident becomes common knowledge around the school. Articles have appeared in two school newspapers, the official high school newspaper and an underground one. This, in turn, stimulates an article in the local newspaper which uses the two high school stories to publish a tongue-in-cheek article meant to be humorous.

Of themselves, the articles are innocent attempts at a man-bites-dog story, but the high school and local news stories have come to the attention of Dr. Malone. I had been noticing an increased interest in and scrutiny of me on the part of the doctor. At the times of my injections, the talk of bazookas and machine guns had ceded to probing questions concerning what I knew about mathematics and questions concerning the mechanics of Down Syndrome and its amelioration. I answer these monosyllabically with my tongue slightly protruding, disclosing as little as possible. From his subsequent looks and behavior, I'm skeptical of the effectiveness of my subterfuge.

On the way back from a playgroup session, my mother makes the statement, "Dr. Malone is suspicious of members of your group. Believing that you're holding back on the gains you all have made. He's called me a number of times, and he sees you as one of the instigators."

"He's just still angry over the laptops," I say, trying to change the subject.

"No, I don't think so. And Mason, he is right, and I'm not sure it's necessary. You're making enemies, first Mr. Meanan and now Dr. Malone. It may not be worth it. I've made you a promise, and I'll keep it, but I'm beginning to question the wisdom of this approach."

I sit there chastising myself, realizing what a mistake my intermediate calculus research has been.

"Mama," I answer seriously, "what do you think would happen if people realized that there are 15 people, former tards," she winces at the term, "that are far more intelligent than some of the smartest people on earth? Also one out of every 100 live births is a Mongoloid, someone with Down Syndrome," I amend. "Further, millions with Down Syndrome can all be transformed the same way we have. That alone represents a significant threat to the status quo." I look at her seriously through the epicanthic folds of my eyes. We are at a stoplight, looking at each other. She lowers her eyes from mine and is silent. "If we let Typicals know the extent of the effects of the therapy, it would result in a revolution of how society is organized. Do you think that those in charge would stand for that restructuring of who's in power, or do think it might be to their advantage to end the therapy and us along with it?"

My mother is quiet for a long while before replying. "But you will need Dr. Malone in the future for those changes."

"No, we won't, we've already synthesized the chemical used in the therapy."

"How?" she asks, clearly amazed.

"One of us has parents who are chemists, and she has secret access to their home laboratory." I tell her about the *Human Genetics* journal, Dr. Malone's first article, and the formation of the group on biology, genetics, and Down Syndrome itself.

"I've read his articles, and while I'm no biologist, there's nothing overt that identifies the chemical," my mother replies.

"That's true, but we figured it out from clues embedded in Dr. Malone's articles, as well as a more extensive review of gene therapy studies."

"We figured it out?" she repeats my words. "How do you know you got it right?"

I swallow, shake my head, and say, "Do you remember when we were in Dr. Malone's office, and he was called out of the office? It was about three weeks ago. When he left, I took one of the injections that were set out for the others. I put it into my jacket and gave it to the chemistry group. They synthesized it, and our results were consistent. We no longer need Dr. Malone."

My claim that we are far more intelligent than the smartest people on earth (maybe not all of them, but most), and certainly all of the world's political and economic leaders, is not totally hubris. We are given all sorts of tests as part of the study, which we go to great lengths to dull down, but we needed a test to tell us what our true abilities are when compared with those of Typicals. This problem is solved by Polly, whose mother is a psychologist. Polly creates an online version of the WAIS, the *Wechsler Adult Intelligence Scale*, the standard IQ test. Each of us has taken this test, in the presence of another Attilian, a name we've adopted for group members. We've taken this precaution due to our increasing sophistication with deception. We now have developed a limited capacity to lie, a consequence from our need to disguise our ever-increasing abilities.

The test tops out with an IQ of 200; only a few people in history have ever approached this score. While there is some historical and clinical ambiguity, a score below 70-80 is deemed to be mentally retarded. Tards are then separated by roughly 20-point intervals into three groups: morons historically clock in somewhere between 51 and 70; imbeciles, between 26 and 50; and idiots below 25. (Don't know what happens if you land on 25.) These clinical designations were used up to the 1970s.

Thirteen Attilians achieved scores of 200, one received a score of 180, and one came in with a score of 145. One eighty is thought to be a genius level, while 145 is borderline superior/genius. All pretty good scores when compared with the majority of Typicals.

24

Mosaics

Holly, however, is the 145, and I had monitored her test. I noticed that Holly was not always as quick to catch on to the various technological upgrades of our IT system, and slower to participate in some of our conversations and conceptual revelations. But I didn't care, and I took pleasure in helping her. Still, her retardation was at the borderline edge of genius. However, the disparity between Holly's scores and the rest of the Attilians was a little troubling.

This discrepancy was soon explained by Amy, the crack biochemist and geneticist. Holly was a type of Mongoloid designated as a mosaic. Most Mongoloids are affected at conception with Bad Mr. 21 with a mutation in the sperm or egg, from this, all descendent cells in the body are affected. In the case of mosaics, the mutation occurs somewhere within the course of embryonic development such that only those cells flowing from this mutation will be affected. The extent of affected cells in the body depends upon when in development the 21 mutation occurs.

The effect is that mosaic Mongoloids have some affected 21 cells, and some typical cells; the overall percentages vary. Since Holly had some percentage of typical cells, the effect of the gene therapy was reduced since there was less raw material for the therapeutic interactions.

The 180 genius, John, was also thought to be mosaic, although it had never been established clinically. The realization of mosaic Mongolism seemed to provide an answer to the discrepancy between IQ scores, which were trivial. Amy postulated a caution that it was possible that the gene therapy, so effective with the genes of the extra chromosome, may have a deleterious effect on typical genes. Other than "out-of-the-question" experiments on Typicals, it was not possible for us to understand this phenomenon further. Dr. Malone, however, would soon enlighten us.

Phase III

Awareness and Activism

25

They're Killing Themselves at an Extraordinary Rate

Our accelerated development was almost exclusively focused on increasing our ability to accumulate facts and to foster fluency to manipulate language. All of us had read at least one major dictionary and some of us had read through an encyclopedia or two. This type of learning is what is most rewarded in IQ scores. Our increasing ability to make and recognize connections (generalization and discrimination) lagged a bit behind the knowledge gains (knowing about things). Our skills, that is, knowing how to do things, concentrated on supporting this knowledge with specific actions. So we were in danger of becoming mere analogs of the encyclopedias and dictionaries we were reading. Transitioning from this phase, our next step was awareness.

It is unnecessary to subject the accumulation of knowledge and the skills that support it to critical analysis. Awareness, however, demands it. The

Hegelian triad of thesis, antithesis, and synthesis was a concept we could all define but were unable to use in the beginning. As we progressed, this would change, and our abilities would grow.

Imagine if a baby were born with full language fluency and a universal knowledge of factual information. That baby still would not have the experiences to function in its society. It would need time to understand nuances and mores, to be able to function as a participating member of that culture. It was not surprising that it took us a while to put things together in a critical way—to synthesize information.

Although awareness happened individually to each Attilian at different times, as a group this awareness had its origin with a statement made by Holly. In a discussion of Typicals and their behavior, she asserted, "They're killing themselves at an extraordinary rate."

This statement sparks an incipient awareness of the vulnerability that Typical behavior subjects society to in general. We listen as Holly continues: "They're involved in countless military operations, they're afraid to call them wars. There are widespread disparities in food, health care, and wealth. There is discrimination between people of different colors," at this, we all look at Ron, the only black Attilian, as she continues: "To different religions, different countries, and different groups within them, woman, members of different classes." She trails off and sighs. "It's like they don't know how to be polite." Holly imparts to Typicals a term of derision that she's long been familiar with. "The climate is becoming deadly, sea water is rising as sea ice is melting and encroaching on the land, droughts are increasing, crops are harder to grow in many places, causing famines. Many leaders, particularly in this country, refuse to acknowledge these facts as real. Most troubling." Holly now exhibits a prejudice of her own. "They're allowing the extinction of animals through hunting and habitat destruction, particularly in Africa. Imagine no more elephants, lions, gorillas, and many others." When she's done, she's exhausted.

"That's bullshit," says Logan, supporting Holly's assertions. Holly's observation initiates a spirited discussion of the things we see as examples of inconsistent and inept actions and policies, and the blatant intellectual incompetence of Typicals. It's an awakening, a call for us to apply an emerging collective critical analysis. It's like we've been released from a cage. Our group will never be the same as it ushers us into our next phase of development.

The development of our critical eye has its origin, I believe, with our program of selling short, as an attempt to identify bad ideas in corporate America, and the world, and relates to other aberrant Typical behavior. While we have been making modest economic progress, there is still a long way to go. Our current balance now stands at $60,000. Logan accounts for half of this while we other 14 Attilians collectively are responsible for the other 50 percent. With the development of our critical eye, we triple the amount in a week. Logan is still the most adept, but the gaps between us are less marked. By the end of the study, we have accrued a balance of a quarter of a million dollars. I take great pride in the fact this watershed was inaugurated by Holly—145 Holly.

26

The Awaking of Intellect and Compassion

Holly's observations represented the moment that Attilians began to use their emerging intellects as more than playthings. Until then, we had been accumulating knowledge as an aesthetic that contributed to the beauty of our lives, our dignity and self-respect, but in the face of the gaping deficiencies of Typical society could we deploy our intellect toward anything that would help? The problem seemed daunting with society's refusal to even acknowledge the problems facing them—indeed, making the problems worse while creating new ones. The situation called for action, and we found ourselves with this question: Could we use our intellectual prowess to make a difference?

It was, at the time, a naive realization, embracing a view that solutions would be a simple exercise, but it represented a first attempt to use our intellect as a tool to modify and shape our environment rather than just react to it. I believe that this was as important to us as it was to humans when they learned to make fire rather than just to shepherd it. It represented our first steps as authentic human beings—and it was powerful. Mongoloids the tool makers. Mongoloids the thinkers. Mongoloids the shapers of their environment.

It was inevitable that this new awareness should transform us, and more precisely align Attilians with activism. The social group's discussions increasingly married activism to improving our position within this flawed society. This outlook was not in itself new, but heretofore our attention concerned improving our financial status, allowing us to purchase things to improve our own situation. These new discussions began to routinely address other Mongoloid populations in our actions, to include those who were not part of the study, those who had not received the benefits of Dr. Malone's bazooka blasts. This ushered in a new emotion—compassion.

Holly's outburst had awakened in us a concern for others, and the discussions and emails sent between us contained many references to the plight of Mongoloids and questions of how to combat the effects of this condition, both physically and socially. The major focus was on extending the benefits of the gene therapy treatment.

This concern for others was new to us, despite the fact we all, to some degree, harbored the innate Mongoloid tendency for sympathy. In our pre-gene-therapy history, we had been the recipients of sporadic, and sometimes excessive, compassion, but with the exception of the application of a few hugs, we had never been the dispensers of it. The question became, how could we deliver the bad Mr. 21 therapy to a large number of disparate Mongoloid populations? Amy and her group could not synthesize enough of the chemical to be effective for more than a few people at a time. Even if we could increase the capacity, the number in our immediate region was enormous, totaling in the hundred thousands, not to mention the country or the world. We were confronted with the fact that despite our emerging intelligence and compassion, these were not yet sufficient to solve the problem.

27

The University

The gene therapy study was ending soon, and it would become more difficult to justify our coming together in a social group. Besides, even with our subterfuge, we had achieved gains to the extent that many of us were no longer diagnosable as retarded. This militated, in the minds of the study staff, more social contact with our Typical mates and reduced the need for our social group to continue. This strategy was spearheaded by Dr. Malone and led us to our increasing distrust of the doctor, causing considerable concern. In the midst of our discussions of compassion, we turned our attention toward what should come next after the end of the gene therapy study. For the moment, we abandoned plans to aid other Mongoloid populations in favor of how we could maintain our close contact. Compassion was thus turned upon ourselves, and we were stymied for the first time.

The final days of the study were devoted to a battery of tests meant to establish the effectiveness of the gene therapy program. This was stressful, as we all attempted to keep the extent of our gains secret. Dr. Malone was ubiquitous during this period, exuding mistrust and frustration and virtually hovering around me. The last test was our old friend the WAIS, the one that Polly had reproduced online and had given us to establish where we fell in relation to standardized norms. My test was administered by Dr. Malone himself. Throughout the test, he tried various methods to expose my duplicity. First, he appealed to my ego, baiting me by telling me I was probably not intelligent enough for a specific section of the test, then changed his tactic and provided me with assurances that he knew I would do well on a specific part, then in frustration told me that he would not include the result of my test in his findings.

Before the test, we had all agreed to try to have our scores fall between 75 and 85, providing Dr. Malone with modest success. I would come in at a cool 76 up from 52. Malone was livid. On the last day of the study and playgroup, I was called into his office. I sat on the opposite side of his desk as he faced me. He was quiet for an uncomfortable length of time, then stood up and, towering above me, hissed, "Tell me about calculus." It was evident that Dr. Malone had come to a different conclusion than had Mr. Meanan. For Meanan, I was a Mongoloid, pure and simple, and could in no way have achieved the results on the calculus exam without chicanery. For Malone, I was a different kind of cheat, withholding the positive effects mediated through the gene therapy. Malone, being the more perceptive, was confused and resented my dishonesty. As a result of his reasoning, he identified me as his adversary.

Answering his query, I replied, "It's a kind of arithmetic."

"What made you think you could enroll in an AP intermediate calculus class?" My indiscretion continued to haunt me.

"I just wanted to take the test," I temporized.

"You got a perfect score on that test. How did you do it?" he thundered over me.

"I just did," I said, gazing off into the dramatic middle distance, my tongue slightly protruding. These simple ploys were ineffective.

"I think you're a liar, Mason Free," he said with his face a few centimeters from my own. I thought for a moment I was about to be struck. To my relief, Dr. Malone gained control of his anger. "Get out of here," he said as he ordered me out of his office.

Subsequently, he wrote my mother a letter claiming that I, and other members of the study, had deliberately withheld the gains of the therapy, for self-serving reasons. However, he was unable to identify what the reasons were. Later, my mother would show me the letter, as his accusations surfaced. The letter seemed more like a rant than a reasoned objection, though Dr. Malone's suspicions were spot-on.

We still have no solution to the maintenance of the Attila group. We are further frustrated since this on the surface seems to be a simple problem. While we can meet as friends, most of our families still define us as retarded. It is apparent that we have not gained the trust that would enable us to associate independently as a formal group, and certainly not on a regular basis.

I keep at the problem, coming up with a variety of scenarios, none of which seem practical. Then, out of ideas, I go back to Dr. Malone's original grant application. The application appears on my mother's official education department website. As I read through it, I recognize the components of our six-month experience. While not speaking specifically to my problem, Dr. Malone has adhered faithfully to the grant protocol. I have to admit that the guy is a good scientist. It's not much help until I get to the very last section. The section addressing *Maintaining the Gains of the Study*. In this section he talks about how the results can be fostered after the end of funding. It's pretty weak when compared with other sections, only listing follow-up testing, interviews, some proposed medical evaluations, and linking up with existing organizations. But the section sparks an idea—not linking with existing organizations but becoming our own. A University.

I had never regarded school as a positive force in my life; because of this, I had not been inclined to see any kind of school as a solution to our problem. But as a means to continue the Attila Group, it offered promise. What if we had a place dedicated to our social group and its activities, under the umbrella of an educational institution? We could continue to meet and evolve, it could even be a vehicle for bringing in other Mongoloids. As the ideas flowed, I became increasingly excited and remained so up to the next meeting of our social group. There, I explained my idea, and members received it with enthusiasm.

I explain it would be a legitimate school, a university where we could gather on a daily basis, pursue our own studies, and collaborate on academic projects and social actions. Most nod and smile. A few, however, say, "I hate school, I can't wait until it's over." They're quickly convinced that it won't be like our current schools, and I get the go-ahead to involve my mother, now considered an ally by our group. With this support, I go to her.

She listens calmly as I make my pitch over dinner at our kitchen table. I tell her that an educational institution would allow us to maintain regular contact with each other and allow us to transform our inadequate schooling into something relevant to our current needs. It takes me almost a half hour to present my multifaceted and often meandering argument, until I run out of things to say.

"Interesting idea, Mason," is her first response followed by a long period of quiet while she thinks. "One problem I see is funding." I know that she believes I'm asking for her to fund the program through her office.

"We have a donor who has pledged a quarter of a million dollars for the initial start-up, with more promised once we are established," I say, and I can see this answer is not what she expected.

"Who?" she asks.

"Us," I reply. And I explain our program of selling short.

"You're making that kind of money accessing the bad ideas of industry and government?" she says, this time incredulous.

"Yes, we're all involved. It was Logan's idea. His fucking idea," I amend.

"Mason!" My mother sounds shocked, and I explain about Logan and his predilection for slang and profanity, and she seems mildly appeased. I haven't realized until then just how disruptive and powerful Logan's language is.

It takes a little time for my mother to wind down from "fucking idea," but she returns sluggishly to the proposal. "How do you think we should proceed?"

I had prepared an outline of the things we should do. "We need a physical place where we can meet, an official designation as an educational institution, and an affiliation to give us credibility and cover. We are hoping to affiliate with your office. We can handle the corporate organization and paperwork to become a legitimate nonprofit foundation," I say. My mother is nonplussed, as she begins to understand the scope and potential of our group. It was a lot for "just a mother," even one running an important governmental educational department, and I leave the ideas to incubate in my mother's expanding understanding of our potential.

28

My Father

I've recounted my collaborative relationship with my mother but said very little about my father. William Free is a well-known and respected conservative columnist who writes opinion articles for the *Washington Post*. His articles and columns are syndicated, which means other newspapers routinely publish them. Because of this, my father exerts great influence, particularly on the political point of view termed the right wing, or conservative wing. Conservatives don't like change, and they don't like progressive ideas, policies, or social programs. What conservatives conserve, mostly, is the status quo. Radical or revolutionary ideas, and what flows from them, are viewed as dangerous. This fear of change is not the best starting point for a deeper understanding of my current transformation. Thus, I'm skeptical about divulging anything concerning my transformation honestly to my father.

His conservatism is not only professional but also bleeds into his personal life; this, I think, was responsible for his opposition to my participation in the gene therapy study. He just doesn't like change. Potential benefits are always outweighed by stability, again not a good starting point for a candid relationship. My father was well-educated in Ivy League prep schools and universities, his language is formal and precise, and his arguments strongly structured, even if often ill applied. He is inflexible when it comes to changing his mind once he's made it up, and his focus is narrow. I believe, but don't actually know, that his inflexibility was a major contributing factor to his divorce with my mother.

Recently, I have read many of his columns in the *Post*'s archives. Almost across the board I find my father's ideas to be short-sighted, sometimes selfish, and flat wrong. This harsh analysis does not negate the fact that my father loves me unconditionally. This love is deep and genuine. In my readings of my father's columns, I found one written when I was seven, just prior to his breakup with my mother, and the column was about me. It related what a charming and significant person I was, stating that I had all the qualities that made a human being human, and that I had these qualities in abundance. His language was equally formal and precise as in his other columns, as he advocated for acceptance and against notions of prejudice in the meaning of pre-judge. It was a warm and loving article, filled with emotion not present in his other writings. He ends the article with an account of a baseball game we had recently attended to reinforce the advocacy. "Mason watched in anticipation, genuinely excited as the runner on third tagged up and scored on a one-out fly ball."

When I read this, I had a strong pang of guilt. My mother knew I was learning quantum mechanics and selling the stock market short, and my father thinks I'm just learning to read with the swinging phonics monkey. After my discussion of the university with my mother, I decide to take a small chance with my father and show him a little light under the door and illuminate some of my nascent development.

That evening after dinner, we're in the living room watching a TV news show. I say, "I read your column about me."

He reacts in surprise. "How?" This is becoming a favorite word shared by both my parents.

"I looked it up in the *Post*'s archive," I answer evenly.

"The *Post*'s archives?" he echoes. "How?"

"I searched it out on my laptop." When we all were given laptops by the study I moved the one I had at my mother's, to my father's house, replacing my tablet. My mother approved the move even though she had originally bought it, saying, "It's your laptop, Mason."

I wasn't sure what was more disconcerting to him, the information I was sharing, or the matter-of-fact way I shared it. After he has processed each of these things, he says tentatively, "What about it?"

"Well," I say, "you argue for me to be incorporated into the hearts of strangers, and into society in general."

"Yes," he says, waiting for what would come next.

"Well," I continue, "in your other columns, you consistently argue against society's role in advocating and funding social change."

He sits in his chair with his mouth moving but making no sound, the light under the door illuminating his understanding. He is holding the remote, thinking of changing the channel when I begin our conversation. He now sets the remote on the coffee table before him, stands up, and leaves the room. I don't see him again until breakfast.

29

Mongolians in the Woodpile

I talk to my father very little the next morning while he continues to think through the implications of last night's conversation. My mother picks me up and delivers me to school. I'm disconcerted as I enter to see Dr. Malone through the window of Vice principal Meanan's office. Meanan's scrutiny has not lessened, and despite the humorous newspaper articles, or perhaps because of them, he has kept up his investigation. If he has linked up with Dr. Malone, my life is about to become more complicated. One good thing is that only one other student in the study attends my school. His name is Scott, and we are not close. But after the Malone visit, Meanan interviews him. I quiz him at the next social group, he says he was asked about how I achieved a perfect score of the calculus test. "I said, 'What's calculus?' Don't worry, he got nothing from me." Scott smiles, and I feel less anxious.

When I'm picked up from school, my mother informs me that the university idea was angrily dismissed by Dr. Malone, who wanted no part of it. He suggests that smaller groups be set up in our home schools and he would agree to supervise them. "For your university to be sanctioned by my office as an extension of the study, we would need the support of Dr. Malone, who is the primary investigator." I am relieved to hear that Dr. Malone is not interested in participating in the university; it would be like hebetating with a spy, and we would not agree to anything that continued our interactions with the doctor. I communicate this to my mother.

"You know, Mason," she continues, "that you don't' need to be an extension of the study to get your school going. You can proceed on your own. My office has some small start-up grants, the funds are minimal, but you have your own funding. When you get your corporate designation, you can apply for one of these grants. That would give your school legitimacy and an affiliation with our department."

"Good idea, Mom," I say, becoming excited again.

I bring the idea to the next meeting of the social group and relate how we would be independent from Dr. Malone and the study, and from anyone else for that matter. The idea is immediately embraced by Logan's "Fuckin'-a, brother, I never did like that douchebag." The others voice their agreement.

Amy exclaims, "We could bring in other Down Syndrome people." Holly adds we could also assist organizations serving Down Syndrome individuals.

The first order of business is to set up our nonprofit corporation. A girl named Susan, whose parents are both corporate attorneys, has been researching the process. She is designated to act as our lawyer and statutory agent. She has already printed out the necessary forms to have them on hand, and we collectively begin the process of filling them out. "The first step is to decide on a name for the organization," Susan says.

"The Mongolian Cluster Fuck," chirps Logan energetically. We employ our emerging critical awareness to table this suggestion. "It is an accurate description of our makeup," Logan defends himself cheerfully. "What about Mongolians in the Woodpile?"

Though the proposal is meant to be jocular and rhetorical, Holly responds reflexively, "That's a racial slur, I think that that's an odious suggestion, and you should know better, what with all the study and discussion we've had about civil rights and history." Holly's reaction highlights two things: The first is a growing sense of morality, history, and political correctness, and the second is our increasing vocabulary. *Odious?* Holly!

"I didn't mean it as a butt-fucking racial slur," responds a defensive

Logan, who had taken a major role in our discussions of the history of the American civil rights movement, "Sorry. But it's like Huckleberry Finn, and the use of the N-word," he adds in his only known instance of political correctness. *N-word!*

This interaction briefly derails our attempts to name the university, replacing it with a spirited discussion of race and recent transgressions with the shootings of black men, women, and children. "They even shot a 12-year-old ba-ba-boy in a public park because he was playing with a plastic machine gun," says Andrew. A few Attilians give other current examples of racism from the news.

"Really fucking sorry," reiterates a penitent Logan.

Back to the name discussion, John suggests the Attila Group, and the ever-cautious Charles responds that we should keep our name for ourselves secret. Besides, he adds that it includes an important word in our security password. Again, this is voted down. There follows a passionate discussion of a variety of suggestions. Holly suggests the Elephant School. "That's lame," responds Logan, "people would think we train elephants." There is no hint of retaliation for the woodpile discussion, and Holly acknowledges the logic of his statement.

In my readings on the history of Down Syndrome, I learned that it was described by the British doctor, John Langdon Down, who first employed the word Mongoloid to describe our condition in 1866. I explain this and suggest Langdon University as an innocuous and somewhat classy name that would alert no one to our subversive agenda. A few more names are offered, but in the end, we adopt Langdon University with its oblique reference.

We then move on to choosing officers and incorporators. Susan says we need a minimum of four, and after an extended discussion the vote is: Charles president, Amy vice president, me as secretary, and Susan as treasurer. While we are all below legal age, Susan informs us that it will probably go unnoticed. Also, we have my mother running interference for us. The rest of our group is listed as directors at-large.

The next order of business is to draft the articles of incorporation and to define the goals and objectives of the organization. Susan asks everyone to email her our suggestions for goals, objectives, and activities, with the caution that these should be as short and as general as possible. She will edit these into a draft, and write the bylaws for our consideration, by our next meeting.

We take the next week to wrestle with these questions. Susan, true to her word, fashions the diverse offerings into a comprehensible whole, and we approve them as written. The stated objectives are few: to establish and provide a full-service educational institution that addresses the academic needs of any persons with Down Syndrome; to provide a library and facility to house materials that enhance the school's educational programs; to support additional educational and social experiences for persons with Down Syndrome outside of the school environment; to develop and disseminate educational materials; and to cooperate with other organizations supplying education and care to persons with Down Syndrome. Our goals include the organization and development of a fully accredited school up through high school and a postsecondary educational program for persons with Down Syndrome, and the activities that support it.

Susan then delivers the good news: As soon as the forms are filed with the Internal Revenue Service, we will be allowed to function as a corporate entity even while we await the final approval. We would be liable for all taxes accrued if denied, but once the forms are in the mail, we are good to go.

"Free at last, free at last, thank God almighty we are fuckin' free at last," are Logan's final words as we disband for the day. I think that Logan's penchant for obscenity and irreverence stems from deep feelings linked to his notions of the failures of a free society to embrace all of its citizens. Joyfully, I revel in the thought that the Mongolians in the woodpile have just been turned loose.

Profile: Logan

When I first met Logan, he was on the cusp of thirteen, one of the younger participants in the study, but indeed its most colorful, not only in his language but also in his candor and in the creativity of his ideas.

He was born to parents in their midlife, his mother's pregnancy putting her at a moderately high risk for giving birth to a mongoloid child. She was well educated and taught English and creative writing at a local community college; she always harbored a bit of guilt for giving birth late in her life. This guilt, however, translated itself into an environment of acceptance and love.

Logan's father was a physician, a gynecologist, described by Logan as a "cunt peeker." Despite Logan's nomothetic references, such as "the old cocksucker," his father was a brilliant physician at the top of his field. Although he had delivered perhaps a dozen Down Syndrome children, upon Logan's birth he set himself to the task of revisiting what he knew of the condition. In his research, he discovered one, and only one, thing that gave him pause—the word *passive*. Low intellectual ability and health issues he could deal with, but not passivity. And he embarked in a war with all things passive. Early on, Logan's initial resistance to having his diaper changed was reinforced by his father, as was all resistance to almost anything. He deliberately set up obstacles, physical and intellectual, that his son had to overcome. All instances of exerting his independence was encouraged, often to his mother's frustration. Logan's character was largely informed through his father's challenges.

An example of his father's influence from his early life I found insightful was Logan's dealing with picture puzzles. His mother was using puzzles to develop Logan's cognitive ability, to foster his language skills and encourage his attention to the detail required to put the puzzle pieces together. On one occasion, while they worked on a puzzle at the kitchen table, Logan turned the puzzle with the pieces picture-side down. He then picked them up assembling them upside down outside of the puzzle frame. His mother sought to correct him, when his father, who had been looking on, intervened with a firm "no." From then on, Logan never again assembled a puzzle picture-side up, abandoning the frame. His father was particularly pleased when Logan started assigning names to the individual pieces. His mother finally took pride in her son's eccentric ability.

Logan's father's war on passivity proved successful; in school, Logan moved from one kind of trouble to another, causing his father to attend countless parent teacher conferences that, in the end, resulted in Logan's placement in a radical open school in a rural farm setting in the Virginia countryside, where Logan contributed to the non-traditional atmosphere, curriculum and community. *Passive* was never a word used to describe him.

In addition to his mother and father, Logan lived with an older sister, who was always a bit ashamed of her brother. There evolved a relationship of antagonism between the two, buffered by a sibling affection, that at best expressed itself as an uneasy truce. She was grateful when Logan moved to the farm school. As Logan's abilities increased, so did the quality of the pranks he directed at his sister and her "asshole boyfriend"—never malicious, nonetheless awkward and annoying.

In my request for a written statement Logan produced this philosophy of life:

"My whole piece-of-shit life has been one long resistance to the way things are normally expressed and routinely done. Even before I realized it, I was a contrary actor in my approach to this humdrum fucking world. I am, to put it in my current vocabulary, a motherfucking skeptic. So much of the world is bullshit, and a good part of the asshole public eat it with their bullshit spoon. If you want change, you have to fuckin' act differently. I read where Ernest Hemingway wrote that every child should be given a built-in crap detector. Well, for the most part, children and everyone else, have chucked their unused detectors in the fuckin' ash heap of sterile normalcy. The greatest gift I ever got was from my cunt-peeking-doctor father, who had me develop my crap detector and gave me chances to use it. I think the worst thing a person can do is to be boring."

30

Irene

To be free at last in reality, we needed to exit our respective educational institutions for permanent residence at Langdon University, where we would really be free to operate and take our intellectual development seriously. The invention of charter schools had significantly dulled down the requirements for the staff. Still, we would need nominally qualified personnel. This problem was solved by hiring Irene. Irene was a teacher at my school and was the best example of benign incompetence: a well-meaning elderly lady and a completely incompetent teacher, even by the attenuated standard of my pathetic school. Irene, despite her challenges, was a real sweetie. She insisted we call her by her first name, violating the school policy of Mr., Ms., Mrs., and Dr. She was a loving person. She often talked to herself, and regularly forgot the names of her students, though she always knew who we were. In short, Irene was the perfect executive director for Langdon University. She was a certified teacher since the 1940s, was undeniably an adult, and was not a

Mongoloid. All important qualities for the public operation of the school.

I suggest Irene to the group and am given the authority to recruit her. For this, I engage the help of my mother, who smiles and chortles as I tell her of my selection and the reasons for it. My mother knows Irene casually from school open houses. "Masterful" is her comment. She smiles as she assures me of her assistance.

Langdon University's first expense is the salary we allocate to our executive director, who as a result receives a $30,000 pay increase, completely covered by the last weeks' selling-short revenues. The second expense is rent on an old brewery refurbished to house a defunct charter school. It is a historic gothic building in Alexandrea, Virginia, which we will end up buying.

"Where's the motherfucking vampires?" is Logan's comment when he first sees the building. But the space is a real find: it has thirty rooms, some of them quite large. It also has gas, water, and vacuum lines installed for use in scientific laboratories. The previous occupants have even left several science tables and chemical hoods. Our executive director signs the lease. So, in a short period, we have our school campus and an executive director to "direct" it.

31

Bad Mr. 21's Revenge

Vice principal Meanan's and Dr. Malone's investigations have revealed nothing, and Malone is increasingly frustrated. He has written a number of letters: to my mother, to her superiors at the Department of Education, and to various members of the medical and scientific community, including the board of the journal *Human Genetics*, accusing the subjects in the study of withholding the extent of benefits of the therapy. He is, however, at a loss to explain our motives. With each letter, Malone seems more unhinged. My mother has taken regular calls from him, each one more frenetic than the last. When he finds out about the existence of the university, probably from Mr. Meanan via the exit of Irene, he goes ballistic and tells my mother that he's tired of being a voice crying in the wilderness and is taking matters into his own hands. This mildly upsets her, as she doesn't know what to expect next. Soon, it will become unfortunately clear.

I am aware of the subsequent developments only in segments. The first

I hear of anything is when Vice principal Meanan accosts me in the halls of the school, saying, "Are you satisfied now, Free? Dr. Malone is critically ill, and you're responsible." He leaves me in the hall under the questioning eyes of surrounding students and teachers. No one makes a move to clarify Meanan's statement, and as the students disperse, I go to my class puzzled. There's nobody at school I can even ask. So I go to the library and take the chance of being seen reading a newspaper. I search it for any information and find a small article saying that prominent American University professor of medical genetics, Dr. Connor Malone, was found unconscious in his apartment by his wife when she returned home from work. Cause is unknown. The article ended with Malone currently at University Hospital in critical condition. Nothing to explain Meanan's odd accusation. I'd have to wait for my mother to pick me up. Maybe she would have some information.

My mother is clearly upset and keeps the story close to her vest; she knows more than she's willing to share. She admits to me that she is aware of Dr. Malone's illness, and that there are others who are also affected, then she says that she is not free to share more of the story. "Mason," she says quietly, "you'll just have to trust me on this. When I know everything, I'll tell you, but this thing has to play out."

She's very interested in my interaction with the vice principal and asks me twice what he said. "He said that Dr. Malone was critically ill and he hoped I was happy since I was responsible." After asking me to repeat it, she looks angry but remains quiet. We don't speak again on the trip home, and it's a pretty silent evening. I log into our Internet chat room, but I'm primarily spreading news rather than receiving it.

Our group spends the next week talking about the organization of Langdon U. I scour the newspapers for any articles about the doctor and his condition, and I learn that it looked as if he had been injected with an unknown drug and had an adverse reaction. Three others of his staff were also affected: Sally, Theresa, and Ted. In a later article, I would learn that Ted, Holly's and my first teacher, had died. The remaining three were still critically ill.

My mother is uncommunicative over the next week, although she did pay a visit to Vice principal Meanan, and seemingly, in the vernacular of Logan, "cleaned his mother fuckin' clock." I don't know exactly what she said to him, but as a result his scrutiny of me stopped along with the investigation.

Two weeks have passed since my encounter with the vice principal, and one more person—Theresa—has died. Sally and Dr. Malone seem to be regaining consciousness slowly. As a group, the Attilians are working on accreditation as a charter school of the state of Virginia. It's a pretty perfunctory process. We work on a small grant through my mother's shop, asking only for transportation funds for our members—bus money, in effect. It's only a few thousand dollars, modest by any standard; we expect no problems getting approved. But it will give us an affiliation with my mother's governmental office.

My mother finally breaks her silence about Dr. Malone and his colleagues, dead and alive. We are at home and have just finished dinner. "I know you've been anxious about the conditions of Dr. Malone and the staff of the behavioral clinic," she says, and I notice she does not use the term *playgroup*. "I think I know enough now to tell you the situation and give you a warning, and it will soon be common knowledge, and in all the newspapers anyway. I know you've been avidly searching the newspapers for information. I also learned some things from your vice principal."

I remain quiet and listen attentively. "As you know," my mother begins formally, "Dr. Malone rightly suspected that you were holding back the extent of the gains you made from gene therapy. He suspected that he had stumbled upon a method of increasing human intelligence and was growing increasingly frustrated that his work was being thwarted. He shared this suspicion with your vice principal, who already knew something funny was going on but had no idea what. As their joint investigation increased its intensity, Malone wrote a number of letters to the Department of Education, the National Institute of Health, the *Human Genetics* journal, and the American Medical Association, as well as a few others, each letter sounding more preposterous than the last, until he was coming to be viewed as a hysterical crank. Do you know the word crank?"

I assure her that I do.

"Finally, feeling out of options and realizing that he was losing status in the field, he injected himself and three other willing participants with the gene therapy chemicals. He was so sure that he was correct in his suspicions. The FBI has retrieved his lab book where he describes the experiment. His colleagues speculate that the injection was so toxic to people with a normal genetic complement that the effects showed up after just two injections. It seems that without the extra chromosome, the result was loss of consciousness and attending coma. If members of your group are beginning to synthesize the therapeutic chemical, you should know you're flirting with potentially lethal side effects."

My assurance that we are, indeed, being careful does not assuage her worry. But her words certainly clarify the mystery. My eyes fill with tears of guilt that my own actions had contributed to this tragic situation. Maybe Meanan was right.

When I inform the group, the first social group at the brewery, Amy tells us that was what the biochemical group had concluded. Amy, et al., had been working on a way to dissolve the injections in water and deliver them in the general water system, and this procedure obviously had to be scraped as far too dangerous for Typicals, but it would allow us to administer the therapy orally to new students.

32

Harold & Irene

The weeks passed; our charter was accepted as written, our certification as an official charter school was approved, and our mini-grant was in the works. The designation as a charter school was important since it allowed us to transfer to Langdon University from our previous schools, where we could avoid stultifying boredom and interact directly with each other every day. My mother took a role in telling the parents that a generous donor had made an excellent special school available to graduates of the gene therapy study. All the Attilians made impassioned pleas to their parents, and all but one agreed. This one, however, was an important part of our plans—Amy. Amy's parents were elated by her gains and were worried about anything that might disrupt her progress. They were unaware of how Amy and her colleagues had gerrymandered their home laboratory. Discussions between Amy and her parents went on for about a week, until my mother put in a call guaranteeing the legitimacy and benefits of the institution. We were whole again.

After our monthly rent of $10,000 and Irene's salary was paid, we still had funds totaling over a quarter of a million dollars. We bought a small used school bus to take the students to and from the school, and my mother's grant would be used toward the cost, but we felt no need to wait. We christened the bus St. Irene's Special School to avoid curious looks. That left just one problem—a bus driver. It would have been perfect if Irene could have driven the bus, but we all felt this would have been too much for the elderly woman. She, however, was central to the solution. As it turned out, this seemingly frail, dotty, sweet woman had herself a boyfriend by the name of Harold. Harold had been a bus driver for over twenty years with the Georgetown School District; this was how they met and fell in love. Irene had a pension from her deceased husband, which was why they never married, and their love never faded. Harold had retired two years previously to spend more time with Irene and so was available to us. Perfect. Harold was an able bus driver, and as oblivious as Irene, oblivious to all but Irene. Their affection for each other was both touching as it was consuming. We pretty much went about our business in anonymity, with Irene checking in on us periodically, asking if we wanted lemonade, tea or coffee, sugar cookies, or various quiches and casseroles she served up from our fully appointed kitchen.

Our first order of business was to develop and equip a fully functional biochemical laboratory and take delivery of a number of top-of-the-line computers. These two projects nearly depleted our funds, but more was coming in with the selling-short project; there remained no dearth of bad ideas from which to build, but given our expenditures, we were interested in developing other revenue streams.

We turned our attention to software development. Logan invented an app that inserted slang and profanity into existing texts. The idea was that you typed in a text of any length, tapped the "fuck it" button, and the app would insert a variety of colorful words or short word combinations in appropriate places. There was even a selector labeled: fuck, motherfucker, and cunt, to set the level of intensity you wanted interjected. Logan had developed it for use with text written by authors that needed a little spicing up, but then an anonymous user got the idea to use existing written material and submitted the Declaration of Independence and the Gettysburg Address for the juiced-up treatment. These went viral on the Internet. From then on, sales went through the roof, and the app was used less as a literary tool and more as a party game. In the three weeks that the software was on the market, Logan had increased the Attilian account to over a million dollars. Between the software and his selling short, Logan was our golden goose. Our 13-year-old Mongoloid golden goose.

33

A New IQ Test

Polly, our resident psychologist, was unhappy with our mostly monolithic test scores and had worked to develop a new test that would result in more variability in the ultimate scores. She was satisfied with the quantification of intelligence but homed in on Holly's treatment of compassion, and she developed a series of questions that measured compassion, and empathy, this along with an analysis of world events such as wars and conflict, views on the treatment of women, global climate change, habitat destruction, extinction of animal species, and views on the equality of various groups. While many of the categories had historically been interpreted as opinions, Polly took a more authoritarian stance and gave values to each answer with respect to its moral position. We all took Polly's new rendition, which mixed sections of the old test with her new assessment, and the results were surprising. She continued to use 200 as the perfect score but balanced the weight of the previous intelligence part with the new test material.

Instead of the near homogenous 200 scores, we all came in a range of 130 to 199, an unexpected diversity. Previously, we all seemed to be in agreement and functioned as a copasetic unit about most all things, but this alerted us to the fact that we were individuals with a substantial within-group variation. With this new revelation, we would hereafter view ourselves as a collection of individuals, not as the previously supposed homogenous band. Differences would surface with respect to our preferences of how Mongoloids should integrate with Typical society and the roles we should play. While this caused me some angst about our future harmony, I was delighted that Holly came out near the top at 189. I, for some reason known only to Polly, came in at 199, the next closest being Amy at 193 followed by Holly. Polly, of course, could not be tested.

Profile: Polly

Polly was born as a first child to a young couple. Her father was a pharmacist, her mother a psychology doctoral student. Her mother looked forward to Polly's arrival and scripted grand scenarios for her unborn daughter, and thus was initially devastated by her disability. Her parents had not performed an amniocentesis or other prescreening activities, their ages putting them in low-risk categories for birth defects. Thus, Polly's unexpected birth condition shattered her mother's projected scenarios. To her credit, she rewrote her expectations for her daughter, changing her psychology field from behavioral psychology to psychometry, the latter dealing with the science of psychological measurement, and vowed to modify the pessimistic predictions made by her conservative professional colleagues. Polly's mother's chief weapon consisted of a variety of psychometric tests and measures. Polly became her mother's laboratory.

She writes:

> *"From as early as I can remember my mother's and my interactions consisted of varied tests and procedures, both formal and informal. Early on, I was tasked with manipulating a plethora of objects that had to be assembled, separated, grasped, or released. I was shown various body movements to be imitated, or initiated on my own. As I got*

older, these objects ceded to cards to be sequenced, identified as the picture that didn't belong, stories to be explained, peg boards and tiles that called for certain actions, timed tests to copy texts, and symbols or pattern to be duplicated. The different forms of these tasks seemed to be unlimited. But I didn't mind, for me growing up, these sessions were an intimate time spent with my mother. The tasks were always presented positively and I thought they were fun; the source of much reinforcement and mutual affection. Subsequent genetic testing revealed that my mother carried what is called a translocation, which meant that the extra chromosome 22 was tacked onto and carried by another chromosome, greatly increasing the risk of the birth of another Down Syndrome child. Not being willing to abort an affected fetus, my parents chose not to have any more children. I've always had my mother's full attention.

"As I developed, I would create new forms of the tasks used to increase my functioning and administered them to our pets, I had a cat that could shake hands, do back flips, speak on command and kiss the dog. The dog exhibited a variety of tricks including petting the cat who was taught to tolerate it.

"So it was natural after the gene replacement therapy that I was well-prepared to quantify the ability of all of us so we could compare it with the so-called normal population, and then to extend the utility of these psychometric procedures to include social and moral dimensions. My interactions with my mother were always about love, as are my new tests, extending the scope and meaning of intelligence."

34

Concern for Others

While the small grant funded by my mother's department was a source of legitimacy, it was also a source of inquiries from other prospective Mongoloid participants whose families were interested in more information about Langdon University and its educational programs. These inquiries originated from the department's website, which provided a short profile of each funded recipient. While in the past we had had discussions of extending the benefits of the gene therapy to others, this was a new direction for us, for Langdon wasn't a real school in a traditional sense, but a gathering place where we could continue to develop our newly acquired abilities and plan for the future. The prospect of bringing others into our group was disconcerting and prompted many discussions—discussions that began to reflect diverging sensibilities.

The curriculum, if there even was one, primarily allowed us to work individually or in small groups (such as the biochemistry group) to learn things necessary to carve out a place in existing society—all while keeping our heads down. Taking in others would make this more difficult and required a structure beyond Irene's tea and sugar cookies. Since the first awakening of our intellect, we had always had the idea of helping other Mongoloids, but these ideas were kept to the back of our mind. These new inquiries brought this issue to the forefront.

Amy had originally planned to make the gene therapy water soluble and put it into the drinking water of various schools and organizations serving Mongoloid populations. While she and her group did manage to make the gene therapy deliverable by water, the lesson learned from Dr. Malone's experiment on himself and his colleagues precluded its use with Typicals in the general public. A more precise and revised approach would be needed.

Again, it was Holly who voiced a concern. "We have an obligation to share the benefits we derived from the gene therapy with our brothers and sisters with Down Syndrome, and not just keep the benefits for ourselves." Her arguments were persuasive, so we somewhat reluctantly agreed to begin an outreach program that would be both progressive and inclusive. The logistics, however, seemed daunting. None of us incipient geniuses had a long-term solution to the obligation Holly identified. However, we did decide to take in willing and interested students into the university. To do this, we needed to look like a more traditional place of learning so that parents and other family members visiting the school would take us seriously.

We mimicked the organization of our previous school environments by developing instruction in reading and language, social skills development, cooking and domestic arts, and physical education, along with an environmental studies program to account for the science laboratory. We took some of Logan's revenues from his "Tourette's for Everyone" app and converted a large space in the brewery into a gymnasium with basketball and volleyball courts, sets of free weights and exercise equipment, acknowledging that we could all use some physical conditioning. We hired Harold to be our de facto gym instructor. With Harold as head coach and Irene as our headmaster, the cosmetics were thin but in place, and we were as ready as we could be for our first visitors.

Our first scrutiny came from a young family with an eight-year-old boy named Adam, who toured the school. The parents seemed impressed initially but were concerned with Adam being the youngest student in the school. Then they asked about the religious orientation as Adam currently attended a Catholic school. They were disappointed when Irene said there was no religious focus to the program, and ultimately, they decided not to send us young Adam. We dodged this non-secular bullet, but this would not be the case in the future. As Logan would predict, "The fucking piece of shit snake in the garden of Eden will come around to bite us in the ass." But that was to be later.

35

The Ambassador

We are next visited by a young man by the name of Matthew. I say young man because that's what he was. Matt, as we came to know him, was just turning 18 and ready to graduate from high school in Alexandria, Virginia. Graduation is a big thing when you're a feeb, since by federal law people with disabilities are entitled to stay in school until a maximum age of 22, though few actually graduate, and most age out with a certificate. Graduation at 18 meant that Matt had completed the coursework needed to satisfy the minimal educational requirements of the State of Virginia—the Typical State of Virginia. Matt is not a typical Mongoloid (if that's not an oxymoron), he's a mosaic. His features showed few signs of Down Syndrome, and he is articulate and conducts himself with confidence and courtesy.

My mother is there for Matt's visit as an advisory board member, and to augment the presence of Irene. Matt's parents are both elderly on the edge of senility. His father was a long-retired geology professor at George Mason

University. Matt has taken the lead in coming to visit us. His parents seem confused about what they were all doing here. Matt periodically provides them with relevant information and orientation. The father becomes animated when Irene shows them the laboratory; Matt is particularly interested in our microscopes. I catch his eye during the tour, and he smiles at me with what seems a deeper understanding of what the school is all about. I instantly like him. At the end of the tour, Matt says he wants to attend. He doesn't say "go here" but "attend." I look over at my mother and gave her a nod. Despite the confusion on the part of his parents, Matt's in. The decision-makers, Irene, my mother, Matt and parents, agree that Matt will join us two weeks hence, after his graduation. I speak to my mother as the family leaves and ask her to set up a few more visitations in the interim.

After Matt and his family leave, Irene returns to the kitchen, and my mother has returned to her office, and we all meet as a group. Amy is the first to speak. "He's obviously a mildly impaired mosaic so we will have to be very careful with the dosage of the gene therapy. We'll need to go slow, he seems to have a strong makeup of Typical genes. We can use Polly's first IQ test to measure the therapy's effectiveness."

"Are we sure we can safely treat him?" asks Catherine, a member of Amy's biochemistry group.

Amy hesitates before speaking. "I believe so," she answers cautiously, adding that "we will proceed cautiously until we know the effects." She hesitates again. "Our experience with Holly and John suggests that the therapy, as we all had it, was not hazardous to their health, and they received the same dose as the rest of us. So, I'm confident that we can safely treat our new member."

"I think Matt knows what he's getting into, at least that he's not coming into a standard educational environment," I contribute.

"He doesn't look fucking Mongoloid," says Logan.

"Yeah," say a few of the others, slightly derogatorily.

I glance over at Holly, and she's looking at me. "Yeah," I agree, "and that's a good thing. We need one of us who can insert themself into society and act as an agent for us. Perhaps he can even conduct transactions with Typicals and not be identified as one of us. In effect, he could be our ambassador." I look around and see various heads nodding, as the others comprehend the implications.

One benefit of being a bona fide educational institution is that Matt's educational file is forwarded to us by his previous school. This contained his educational history over his last twelve years. Matt's last IQ score was 89, not even in the retarded range, but in the range of "dull normal." After seriously studying Typical society over the last six months, I think this classification is best described by the colloquial phrase "the pot calling the kettle black." Still, probably because he was identified as a Mongoloid, Matt had been enrolled in programs for retards throughout his education. Despite this, he had managed to be enrolled and pass enough Typical courses to earn a place in a graduating class commensurate to his age.

Over the coming months, Amy's low-dose gene therapy transforms Matt in the same way we had all been transformed with seemingly no negative side effects. Matt's educational process mimicked our own—his emerging intellect fostered by the use of a new laptop that we provided to him. As he gained increasing facility, he was able to take an active and creative role in our discussions. He develops a fast friendship with, of all people, Logan, who initiates him into the arcane methods of selling short. They form a collaboration in which Matt shows a distinct flair. Logan proves to be a creative and patient teacher, and Matt an eager and receptive student.

After Matt's successful transition, it was Amy's guarded assessment that genes from Bad Mr. 21, as we all still called it, in some somatic percentage confer protection against the effects incurred by Dr. Malone and staff, while still bestowing the intellectual benefits. As a result of the profile on my mother's Department of Education website, we continue to receive a growing interest from the public, and it is clear that our strategy of dragging our feet is no solution to the wholesale incorporation of other Mongoloid populations.

36

The Parents

Matt's quick and successful transition spawns a number of group discussions concerning expansion of our program to others and the problems this entails. It is testament to the intractability of the problem that for the second time in our cumulative history, no one has any bright constructive ideas. While we have one success, there are literally millions of Mongoloids in our country alone. Even if we could put the therapy into the water system, what would be the result of thousands of tards becoming geniuses overnight? The problem is daunting. On our third group meeting on the topic, everyone is irritated and cranky. Holly then tentatively ventures an idea. "Mason's mom has been crucial to all our achievements: the computers, our university, getting us out of our schools, keeping our secrets, helping to recruit new students, everything. Why don't we let our parents in on some of our new abilities and enlist their help?" We all sit there silently with our mouths open and maybe our tongues protruding slightly.

Holly takes in a deep breath and continues, "Actually, they're already helping with their expertise, albeit not knowingly. Amy's parents are chemists, and she has used their library and laboratory to recreate our gene therapy. Polly's mother is a psychologist, and she has used her testing equipment, materials, and library to construct our IQ tests, Charles' father is an expert in IT, and Charles put together our Internet communications, and John and Andrew's parents are indirectly responsible for our bank accounts. Look, they love us and I don't think it's out of the question to think they can be as supportive as Ms. Free. We can at least expect them to keep our secret." Holly folds her hands in front of her, indicating she is finished.

First to speak is Logan breaking the ensuing silence. "My father will have a cocksucking heart attack, but it's the first progressive motherfucking idea we've had."

I look admiringly at Holly and after a while say, "Holly's made a serious suggestion that we need to discuss. She's right that we could not have gotten anywhere near this far without the help and understanding of my mother. Holly's suggestion could help us out of the funk we seem to find ourselves in."

Charles is skeptical. Being the greatest advocate of our secrecy, saying that even though he has great respect for his father, he thinks that the suggestion may be too radical and dangerous.

Amy is typically cautious but suggests a way to mitigate Charles's concerns. "We could go slow on this and monitor their reactions. Mason was cautious with his mother until she proved to be a supporter. I will need to go slowly with my parents, particularly my dad. It will shatter his world view." She pauses, then says, "But I think it's worth a try."

Heads nod, and in the end, we unanimously vote to go ahead to develop an outline of how we should proceed. Susan, our lawyer, suggests that we continue our discussion via email. She offers to coordinate the suggestions into a draft that we can discuss as a group, and everyone agrees. Harold then pokes his head in the door of our meeting room to say the bus is ready for transport home.

37

The Document

The night's emails have been lively, with lots of suggestions and lots of trepidation. More of the suggestions concern what not to do than what to do. Susan has done a yeoman's (yeowoman's) job, cobbling together a coherent document for us to review. It reminded me of my Rules for being Mongoloid; that seems a long time ago.

Susan had titled the document "Fessing Up," testifying to Logan's influence on our language and discourse.

<u>What Not to Do</u>

Don't let them know the full the extent of your abilities.

Don't use big words and long sentences to describe your progress, or your observations about them.

Don't contradict your parents about things they find obvious or self-evident, even if false. This is particularly true, at first, of arithmetic, higher mathematics or scientific principles.

Do not read with high fluency.

Don't make overt comments or insights about current events, politics, or about your parents' professional behavior.

Don't insist upon increased independence in the beginning.

What to Do

Go slowly in your description of your progress. Present your parents with the milestones chronologically as they happened to you. Take time to tell your story.

Speak with a vocabulary that they are used to hearing, then introduce them incrementally to your increased facility as you think your parents are ready.

Read slowly in the beginning.

Increase your vocabulary at a level commensurate with your parents' ability to adjust to it; the same is true for comments about current events or politics.

Make your parents think that you are learning new things from them. Take your cues from their conversations with others, then ask questions about what you've heard. Ask your parents to explain what they've said. Watch television with them and ask questions. Make them partners in your learning.

Each situation will be different, with some parents coming along quickly and others moving more slowly. Be gentle and realize it's difficult for them to change their ideas of the world.

All of the ideas presented are good. I think about how to employ them with my father, and wonder if they will be enough for him to adjust to more of my abilities. But we obviously need the support of more people than just my mother. What we need are allies and our parents seem to be our best shot. The other Attilians agree, and we begin the campaign to recruit our parents.

38

William Free

I begin fessing up with my father, William Free. I had developed an opinion of his public persona by reading his columns and viewing him on television—he was a frequent pundit on news shows. In these appearances and in his columns, he espoused and defended the conservative point of view. This view was not just about a distaste for change but included advocating for a reduction of the size and scope of government, opposing social programs and the funding to pay for them, supporting the private sector over government, a reduction of almost all regulation, and a measured reluctance to accept climate change. His stance, it seemed to me, was more about the direction of change than it was a resistance to it. It did not necessarily concern conserving anything, but in my view had the effect of squandering resources and distributing them to private individuals and companies.

In my odyssey to bring my father into the ranks of possible historic change, I knew I would have to balance two things: the first was my feelings that he was wrong about almost everything he spoke or wrote of professionally, and second was that he loved me and me him.

He opposed my move from my previous school to Langdon University, saying there was no need for the change. He posed lots of questions and displayed an anger reminiscent of his fight over my inclusion in the gene therapy program. The result of his opposition was also similar to his opposition to the gene therapy program. My mother, after attempts at reason, retreated to the authority of custody.

I begin my velvet assault with a simple statement at dinner, saying, "Dad, I need to tell you that the gene therapy worked far better than you probably think."

He is casually reading the newspaper at the time and looks at me. "How so?" he asks. Over the past months he has adjusted, and been pleased, at what he interprets as a mild increase of my intellect.

"It was far more successful than you suspect," I say flatly. My father, I think, reacts more to my delivery than to my words. He sits up straighter, puts his newspaper down, and looks straight at me.

"How so?" he asks again, adopting his professional strategy of not giving up anything before being sure of his terrain.

"I'm considerably more intelligent than you imagine." I say this, rather than "I'm smarter than you think." I'm counting on his intelligence to override the disorienting aspects to my message.

"Explain," he says as if I were a television opponent.

"Dad, before I can share this with you, I must have your promise to keep our secret—off the record, so to speak, and not to talk or write about what I'm about to share with you."

"Our secret?" He exhales as his first unguarded response.

"Yes, this involves all of the students in the study and now at Langdon University. But before I can share this information, I will need your promise."

"Does your mother have this information?"

I debate my answer. "Yes," I answer truthfully. "She has given me her promise."

"Is anything you will tell me illegal?" he asks cautiously. I'm back to being an opponent on television.

"No," I say, not completely successful at suppressing a chuckle, thinking of the paucity of crimes perpetrated by Mongoloids. I am heartened by the fact that this conversation feels like one, if not exactly between equals, at least one between Typicals.

William Free thinks hard. There is a long and uncomfortable silence during which we look at each other. Finally, he says a little sadly, "Yes, you can trust me, Mason."

"Is that your promise?' I press, putting us back on television.

"Yes," he says.

"OK!" I say brightly, relaxing the heretofore formal interaction. "Do you remember the calculus test that became a problem at my previous school?"

"Yes, the vice principal called me, and I could shed no light on the deceptive incident he thought you were party to. It's evident that he still thinks you cheated."

"Well," I say, "I took the test on my own and passed it with my own knowledge. I did it to test how Typical people would interpret an intellectual achievement by a Mongoloid. It was a miscalculation with what followed, but we all saw the result, and," I add, "the need for secrecy."

"Don't use that term, Mongoloid," he says reflexively. Then, "How?" He is barely audible.

"Dr. Malone's gene therapy program worked far better than even his group had anticipated. Our group has done genetic research and attributed it to two factors, pleiotropy and epistasis."

My father shakes his head in disbelief. I continue, "Pleiotropy concerns the genetic interaction whereby one gene has cascading effects on a number of characters at the same time, and epistasis is where multiple genes contribute to a single effect augmenting a single character."

I can see that my father is near overload, and I feel it wise to back off for the night and let him digest what he has heard. But he continues with a question. "How did you ever pass the calculus test?"

I attempt an explanation. "The gene therapy orchestrated physical changes so that learning and memory became acute; everything I hear, see, observe, and read, I remember and connect. These, in turn, create a symbiosis with my curiosity, which furthers my education and intellect. The educational activities of the behavioral clinic initially sparked our facility with words and numbers. Those of us with computers, or in my case, a tablet, were able to learn to read; you yourself started me off with the swinging phonics monkey. Once I learned to read and developed a vocabulary to understand what I read, the rest was easy. I've literally read thousands of books: technical, literary, and scientific. Mom got me a Kindle. I taught myself mathematics and am currently doing work in quantum mechanics. By the time I conceived of the experiment with the calculus class, I was doing linear algebra. At the point I took it, the test was easy. But no one even entertained the possibility that I had passed it fairly, because no one could look beyond the fact that I'm a Mongoloid."

My politically correct father again reacts to the word, and I tell him that I use it as a heuristic, to make sympathetic people think of our position. He mouths the word "heuristic."

I continue with my account. "Many of the people in our group underwent similar transformations. We all owe a great debt to the swinging phonics monkey. Once Mom arranged for everyone in the group to receive laptops, all of us progressed in much the same way, though our interests, and later, our expertise varied individually."

"Your mother was responsible for your group receiving laptops? That was early on. How long has she known about your abilities?"

I hesitate again, then go with the truth. "Almost from the beginning."

My father takes this information in silence. "Members of our group have all experienced some degree of disorientation and discrimination from family and society with respect to their emerging abilities. All of us agree that it was prudent to keep the most dramatic gains of the gene therapy secret. Dr. Malone suspected a program of secrecy and became increasingly frustrated finally embarking on an unfortunate experiment of injecting himself and a few of his colleagues with the gene therapy agents. He was unaware that the extra genetic material responsible for Down Syndrome" (I figured I'd give him a break) "conferred an immunity, and without it, recipients would undergo significant toxic effects."

"Your mother knew from the beginning," he says, looking to the kitchen door. Without another word, he folds the newspaper he is still holding into quarters, stands up, and exits the room. There are tears in his eyes.

39

Black Eye

In retrospect, all of the Attilians who were an original part of the gene therapy program had evolved together—both intellectually and socially. As such, we were a close-knit group. And it was inevitable that close friendships between individuals would naturally develop. Holly and I were a case in point; while we both felt a close kinship with the group, we felt closest to each other. This was true for many Attilians who formed close bonds between themselves and other individuals. This was the case for Amy and June.

Initially, they came together as part of the biochemistry group, but soon found affinity for each other with interests that extended beyond biochemistry and research projects, often spending their social time with each other. In the beginning of the study, June was shy and reticent, keeping mostly to herself, but under Amy's influence she blossomed into an outgoing youth, engaging socially with others and as a participant in our group meetings. With Amy she was particularly vivacious and engaging, becoming one of the more popular Attilians. This metamorphosis, if we thought about it at all, was attributed to overcoming her shyness and feeling more confident in social and group situations.

June spent increasing time at Amy's house and often spent the night. She developed a mutual relationship with both of Amy's parents, particularly Amy's father, who, having made his peace with Down Syndrome, showed affection to this outgoing and intelligent friend of his daughter's; June often accompanied them on family outings and short trips. The bond between the two girls grew and transformed them more into sisters than close friends.

So, we were all curious when June came in one Monday morning sporting a large and multicolored black eye. The black eye occupied her entire left orbit and extended down to her cheek showing the dominant colors of black, purple, with some yellow at the borders, intruding at places into the dark expanse. Logan was the first of many of us to question the origin of the injury: "You fuckin' take up prize fighting over the weekend? That's one major league shiner." It looked more like a map of an island drawn around the central lagoon of the eye that periodically watered and was painfully dabbed dry with a Kleenex.

"I ran into a door," was her cliched response, coming meekly from behind her Kleenex.

"Doors are either open or they're closed, you don't just walk into a fuckin' door, and even if you do it wouldn't go inside your whole eye socket and around your cheek," Logan pressed.

June answered with more spirit, "The door was partially open, I wasn't looking, and I ran into its edge—that's all." At this point, Amy inserted herself into the interaction. "Leave her the fuck alone," she ordered Logan, with her own epithet, that served to dampen further questions.

"Fuckin' A, I'm just sayin', it's not an adequate explanation." Logan left it there.

Our weekly meeting was starting and Amy took June by the arm and led her into the make shift amphitheater. Although quelled by Amy's reaction to Logan, we acknowledged the veracity of his challenges.

At the end of the meeting, June entertained further, less-combative questions from her concerned colleagues, sticking to her "door" story; Amy kept a protective orbit around her. The consensus was that whatever happened, June was embarrassed to tell. Amy, however, maintained a grim secret. A secret that would change Attilian history forever.

40

Other Parents

Most other members of our group proceed more slowly and are curious about my interactions with my father. They're interested to see the ultimate result of my direct approach. I realize that I have violated the first directive of Susan's document. I'm curious as well; my father has not commented on our conversation in the past 24 hours. I'm a little concerned, but I continue not to soften my abilities in our interactions.

Other experiences of the fessing-up phase are diverse. Logan has chosen what would be the most frequently adopted strategy, by simply behaving around his family in a manner consistent with his abilities. "My parents treat me like a fucking talking couch," he says. "My asshole father even thinks I'm cool. I love that cocksucker."

Other Attilians relate similar, though less colorful, accounts of letting their abilities out of the closet. Most relate positive reactions from their family—siblings are the most supportive, but their parents seem pleased.

Amy is the only one, other than me, to have a direct conversation. She relates an awkward exchange with her father, the famous chemist. "He's quite disoriented by my ability to talk about chemistry, particularly when it comes to a discussion of his latest scientific paper. He speaks haltingly, barely able to get his words out. He asks a few questions, and when I answer with a knowledge of relevant chemical principles, he stops talking. There are tears in his eyes and he ends our interaction by hugging me."

June, the third member of Amy's biochemistry group, shares the only negative reaction to fessing up. "We are at a restaurant, and I begin to read the menu. I am feeling proud of my reading ability when my father angrily snatches my menu away and asks me what I'm playing at. 'I'm reading,' I answer. I expected that they would be proud of me, thinking that I had learned to read at the gene therapy school—I try to explain this—but rather than proud they are hostile. We leave the restaurant without ordering. My father looks around us to see if anyone has noticed. My mother looks at my father and whispers, 'The work of the devil.'"

June's parents, it turns out, are born-again Christians, interpret the Bible narrowly, and live their lives strictly in accordance with their literal beliefs, seeing God everywhere. They seem to view their daughter's transformation as an act against God. We watch this situation closely.

Other than June's experience, the fessing-up program seems to be proceeding positively. The strategy would evolve slowly, resulting in what would transform into various levels of support.

In my case, William Free ends his silence after a few days with the statement, "Mason, I'm very glad of your intellectual progress, but it will take some getting used to. It's like getting to know you all over again." This time there are tears in my Mongoloid eyes.

Phase IV

Lost Innocence

41

Heart Attacks in Harmony

My mother has become the point person for communicating with parents with respect to the benefit of enrolling their children in Langdon University. We have continued to grow our financial resources, which now total in the tens of millions of dollars. We have decided to keep this secret from our emerging parental support, perpetuating the myth of a generous donor. We instead concentrate on our mission and goals, and building support for our outreach programs. But acceptance of our abilities by our parents seems to be increasing. The only fly in our ointment continues to be June's parents. They are high-end real estate agents who somehow manage to keep their religious fervor under wraps in their business dealings. Beyond their professional interactions, her parents are fundamentalist zealots. June tells us that they have had a number of sessions to pray over her. She assures our worried looks that she has, with her colleagues in the biochemistry group, prepared a contingency plan. This, however, does not assure us.

It was not until the changes brought about through gene therapy that June realized the extent of a lifetime of abuse and neglect. Her previous condition of limited intelligence buffered her from the worst of the physical and emotional effects applied to her through the parenting practices that were a routine part of her upbringing. With the advent of increased intellect, these transgressions became apparent to June in a mixture of anger and sadness.

After weeks of indignities following the incident at the restaurant, June asserts herself and tells her parents about a large part of her abilities. "It was reckless, but I just couldn't take it anymore," she says. After her announcement, her father strikes her to the floor of the kitchen. I wonder what it is about kitchens that seem to be the favored milieu for fessing up. After they clean off the blood from her cheek, they declare they are going to their minister and perhaps the FBI, and "spill the beans on your dirty secret and end this evil aberration".

"You remember when I had my black eye? Logan was right, it didn't happen from a door—it happened from my father's backhand slap."

This is how June tells us. "The religiously mediated actions directed toward me, do not bode well for me or the rest of us—it's dangerous. It simply isn't rational to be viewed as a work of the Devil. I raised the issue for discussion with the biochemistry group and, we, over a number of discussions, decided that they might have to die if that was the only way to keep our secret."

This last statement strikes us like a baseball between the eyes. We sit around our circle with our hearts pounding and our mouths open. What any members outside the biochemistry group don't know is that Amy had started to research and developed an expertise with poisons, June now fills us in:

"Amy has, over the last months, developed a water-soluble poison that she felt due to its qualities and uniqueness is probably not identifiable by typical medical procedures. She put together two packets of powder that I carry with me. I hope that I won't have to use them, but I'll accept the responsibly if I have to." June relates this without showing emotion.

Two days later, she tells us: "In the end, I had to. The last straw was a conversation where I overheard my parents planning how they were going to expose us to the FBI. In their words, 'To free the world of this Godless mutation.'

"In addition to their zealous religious activities, they both were zealous runners and ran together every morning before breakfast. I placed the contents of each packet into the orange juice they drank before beginning. They died together on that run with what was identified as heart attacks. I destroyed the paper packets in the garbage disposal."

After June's recital, Amy fills us in on the particulars. "I developed an interest in poisons during the time I was busy synthesizing and modifying Dr. Malone's gene therapy agent. At first it was simply an academic exercise, I never thought of using them, as I created a number of different ones." At this point, Holly interrupts.

"How did you test them?" she asks, concerned that animals might be the subjects. Amy assures her that she didn't, in fact, test any of them, being confident of their effects.

She continues: "Again, I used a biological and evolutionary approach and isolated and modified existing biological agents. I created one from hemlock, but its use on June's parents was not an option as it would be too easily identified. I also did some work with poisonous mushrooms I gathered from the well-watered lawns of the Rock Creek Cemetery. Members of the Amanita species offered the most promise, and through the literature I established its lethal effects occur almost immediately. It is also not usually identified through autopsy, but rather from reports of friends or family members who had observed the events around collection and ingestion. I further modified the chemical to make it less identifiable. I also became interested in the algae causing the poisonous effects of red tide that are transmitted to fish and shellfish. Currently there is an outbreak in the nearby shores of Virginia and New Jersey. I isolated one chemical found in these affected algae and added it to the Amanita modified chemical that I gave to June.

"After June had administered the poison, I joined her at her house and we cooked some fish and added some algal organisms responsible for the toxic compound. We left a small amount of the fish in a frying pan on the stove so it looked like it was eaten at last night's dinner. The algae-derived chemical would be found in both the fish and her parents. After initial suspicion by the authorities, the red tide provided a plausible explanation of their deaths."

I listen to her account along with the others, totally impressed. I vowed never to get on the wrong side of Amy.

"The murders," says Amy, not one for mincing words, "ended a lifetime of abuse and neglect of an innocent daughter, but it was not an act of vengeance or retribution but one to ensure our secrecy—to preserve the survival of our group." Amy closes her oration with a musing from her evolutionary expertise. "June's parents referred to us as a mutation. Down Syndrome, or Mongolism would be more accurately described as a genetic anomaly leading to a physical and mental condition. Mutation along with natural selection are the main driving forces of evolving species, and when I think about it, our bad Mr. 21, along with gene therapy may, in fact, be the next evolutionary step for humans." Most of us present are dumbfounded by the implications of this off-the-cuff observation.

A good many of us had read the newspaper article titled "Heart Attacks in Harmony." The story gave a short biography of June's parents and focused on their professional lives and described how each of them suffered a heart attack literally within seconds of each other (a tribute to Amy's precision). There was no mention of suspected foul play, red tide or otherwise, and no mention of their religious predilections. June was briefly mentioned as a surviving teenage daughter. Those of us who had read the article had given silent thanks for the timely—albeit draconian—solution to the problem posed by June's parents. Little did we realize the cost of this solution.

"I told you religion would come 'round to bite us in the ass," Logan reminds us.

Charles says that June acted bravely. "We could have been shut down before we even began."

I feel that this is a potential watershed moment that could split our group apart and suggest we take a vote to approve June's action, and that of Amy and the biochemistry group. The move is meant to assume collective responsibility. I make this point, and most seem to think this is a worthwhile idea.

We take a vote and everyone approves of the action except Holly. "I just can't," she says simply. I look at her across the circle and she shakes her head at me. If she would have voted first, I don't know how I would have. For the most part, our harmony is preserved, but from here on Landon University and its actions would be built over a foundation of blood.

Profile: June

It was June's misfortune to be born as an only child to parents who were fundamentalists, born-again Christians, if fundamentalist and born again are not oxymorons. To them, June's birth was a judgment from God, a judgment that was not taken well; a constant reminder of some unidentified affront that at least one of them had committed to anger their unforgiving deity. Thus, June was denied a loving family from her beginning. Despite that, June had become a curious and open child, who sought love, and to love in a sterile atmosphere. Her mental retardation was an early benefit to her as she did not understand the epithet "abomination," which her mother constantly wielded. This, along with "unholy," "judgment," "punishment," and "bad seed," were not recognized for what they meant until the time of gene replacement therapy. So, June coasted beneath a benevolent shield of ignorance.

June's parents somehow managed to mitigate their religious fanaticism when dealing with their real estate clients. This strategy led to a lucrative lifestyle that allowed them to farm out June's care to sundry surrogates; this was a blessing, in the more conventional style of Christianity, providing June with an infusion of affection and outlets for mutual expressions of love. The relationship June developed with Amy's parents was the latest example of this benign neglect.

Her mother always wanted another child, but when faced with further judgment from their wrathful creator, the parents declined to engage, and because they eschewed the use of any birth control devices by fundamentalist fiat, took up running as a substitute for sex. The tactic was so successful that June's mother stopped menstruating and after a few months allowed the couple to resume coitus, thereby softening some of the resentment harbored toward their daughter.

School for June was always a joyous activity, exposing her to a variety of social interactions and friends. Her mother, however, lived a joyless existence and resented any source of joy in her daughter, striving to curtail it whenever it surfaced in June's proximity. These restrictions extended to friends and social contacts, and June was discouraged from forming any meaningful relationships with her peers. A bit of serendipity emerged when her parents decided to buy a trendy cockapoo, more as a status symbol than any object of affection. The dog, however, immediately established a bond with June. Her parents, with little affection to give, allowed the two license to interact with each other.

The relationship with her dog, Daisy, nurtured June's emotions until the time of the gene therapy study. Her parents allowed her to attend the study, as they reasoned it could perhaps provide a relaxation of their judgment from God. At the time of the playgroup, the emotionally starved June developed a fast friendship with Amy that would prove to be a turning point for both June and our emerging group. The parents allowed this relationship as it gave them time away from their star-crossed unholy daughter.

Not until the advent of gene therapy, and the development of her intellect, did June began to understand her history, joining it to her unfolding life, its implications, and her future.

She writes:

> *"My parents were pathetic, and I'm still angry. Before the gene therapy program their behavior toward me was mostly a withholding of emotion and affection. After the program, and a recognition of my abilities, their abuse became more physical: and slaps, pushes, and blows became routine aspects of my day. But I feel mostly sad when I think of them now. They were people held captive by a prison of their own creation. In order to have the security religion provided, they sacrificed their lives. Once they must have entertained feelings of compassion and joy. But these they turned over to a joyless and vengeful God that occupied their minds as a ghost in an unforgiving machine. I don't believe in Hell, but their lives were a parody of it. I don't excuse my actions, but their end was a release from a dark confinement. Perhaps, in a universe governed by a more graceful force, they can find Joy and Happiness."*

42

Analogs and Missionaries

In the post-murder phase, we Attilians attempt to regain our prior equilibrium, however tenuous. June, who has no close relatives, is in danger of becoming a ward of the state. It is a result of the friendship developed between June and Amy that June became close to Amy's parents. In the course of their biochemistry activities, and social interactions, June often took refuge in Amy's home during daytime hours. This led directly to a relationship with both Amy's father and mother so that her parents, after discussions with Amy, volunteered to adopt her in the wake of her perceived tragedy.

While our group remains intact, we are no longer the unconditional good guys. Like the theme of much of the literature I've been reading for eight months now (*The Lord of the Flies* comes to mind), we have lost our innocence. Still, we move forward.

We direct our current activities toward legitimizing our curriculum, particularly around our independent access to the community. These represent, for us, a de facto coming out of the closet. The curriculum is now represented by programs in reading and literature, speech, quantitative skills, computer literacy, and natural history and remedial studies. These have become necessary to explain our intellectual expansion mediated through the gene therapy program that by necessity needs to be kept covert. Prospective parents are excited by the dynamic quality of the university, its progressive curriculum, and the gains expected for the new students.

We have structured these programs to include parents and students supportive to our overall goals and objectives, and to discourage parents with religious or reactionary objections to a non-traditional school program. These parents often tended to be fundamentalists, or right-wing religious families. We have inserted phrases into our promotional material that highlight our bias against doctrinaire religion. A class titled Religious Democracy, which emphasizes an equal treatment of the big ideas of the world's religions, has gone a long way to exclude zealots. We've learned our lesson.

As we approach the first anniversary of the gene therapy program, we now have a student body of around 90. To accommodate this number, we have converted one of the previous brewing rooms into a circular amphitheater that resembles a forum. This modification allows us to accommodate all of the burgeoning Attilians, and through their participation maintain our direct democratic model. This model is a bit attenuated since we have formed an executive committee, made up of the original 15 Attilians and Matthew, to discuss and determine directions and policies before bringing them to the general forum. As a group, we are the only ones who know a number of our secrets. The important ones are the murder of June's parents, the extent of our increasing wealth, our history with Dr. Malone, and the importance of my mother in past actions. We also continue to perpetuate the existence of our mythical donor. As a short-term strategy, it proves effective, but will soon breakdown.

One abiding characteristic of Mongoloids is our capacity to keep a secret. I don't know if it's a function of the gene therapy, or something innate to us as Mongoloids, but not one of us, old or new, has betrayed our secrets or our need for secrecy. This is paramount to our future activities as we expand our reach.

Even with the spacious brewery, our ability to bring in new members is becoming stretched to the limit. We've had to hire a new bus driver and buy a second bus. The solution is obvious, once it occurs to us: missionaries—educational missionaries.

I use the term "Standard Mongoloids," or "Standards," to refer to those that are affected with Bad Mr. 21 who have not yet received the gene replacement therapy treatment. Instruction of Standards is routinely done primarily by special education in the public schools. I've previously made reference to these programs, which fall into two delivery systems. Self-contained programs, in which groups are formed entirely of retards and are subjected to a curriculum made up of variants of basic academic skills, music, cooking, P.E., and a variety of courses termed survival skills. These include how not to be burned by stoves or hot water, or how to take the bus and not get killed in traffic. (In my case, after seven years of instruction, I was still working my way through the alphabet and various signs on restroom doors.) Like everything else in the world, these programs run the gamut from excellent to incompetent; from stimulating to stultifying; from promoting independence to de facto incarceration.

The second type of program is considered to be the more progressive and is termed integration and, in its most extreme form, full inclusion. These programs integrate retards of various degrees into Typical classes and make attempts to adapt the curriculum. When done skillfully, this type of program can have liberating benefits, most often social, like making Typical friends and getting invited to Typical parties. When done poorly, they can be bastions of loneliness, with the Standard marooned in an incomprehensible landscape. Even where offered, access to integrated classrooms drops off the higher up the educational ladder you go, being more frequent in the elementary grades than in secondary schools.

In reality, most programs are an admixture of both types. The more well off your parents are, the greater the probability of a better school experience. The Attilians bring a wealth of individual history with respect to the various types of programs, and our Education group has done a good deal of research. As a working group, we're split down the middle between those who are sympathetic to the special education model and the challenges they confront and those who are outright hostile to it in any form. I find myself slightly over the hostile line. Charles is the most vocal critic of special education programs, feeling even before the gene therapy that they were condescending and bigoted, though he didn't yet have the words.

I share some of Charles' antipathy. Those students that I observed in total inclusion in the upper grades functioned much like dancing bears, to use Holly's term, with their program being more important to Typical parents and educators than to the students themselves. Based on my own research and observation, I have taken to term this type of programing as analog programing, in which the student functions merely as an analog of a Typical, dropped into a typical situation or environment.

Holly's observation is: "You can train a bear to walk on its hind legs and balance on a ball, but in so doing, you lose the meaning of a bear. We're just dancing bears to them."

"Take it all around," to quote Huckleberry Finn, special education regardless of its quality is a relatively benign force in the lives of tards when compared with the most common post-school options. At the end of special education, support becomes more perilous for Mongoloids. This phase resolves into two types of options. The first is the day activity program, in which tards are kept busy and to some extent entertained for six to eight hours a day. The second is the vocational program.

To a large extent, a retard is not seen as a person in their own right, but as an inferior copy of a Typical. Education becomes a process of re-creating watered-down experiences. Thus, feebs become analogs or copies of a more authentic type in their various roles. Nowhere, in my opinion, is this analog program more pernicious than in vocational training for retarded adults.

The major role of the individual in society is to have a job, true for both Standards and Typicals, to become a component of a workforce providing a function society deems necessary. The more prestigious term for jobs is vocation, and this indicates a life's work. In the best cases, the work is satisfying. At worst, jobs represent a life of tedium and sorrow, directed only to make enough money to provide for the minimal resources needed to keep one's family alive. Most live somewhere in between: artists, actors, doctors, and captains of industry on one side; janitors, slaughterhouse workers, and coal miners on the other. Whatever the prestige, all these vocations address a legitimate societal function, with some semblance of purpose.

The vocational program, however, is a euphemism, an analog, or shadow, of a genuine job that provides neither meaning nor a significant wage. Employers receive some time-limited compensation for each Standard in their employ. For Standards, it is a shell game in which individuals are moved around in endless circles of meaningless activities and trivial pay. All to keep the compensation coming to the employer; in this, Mongoloids and other tards trade endless tedium for little reward.

Why, then, is this the most coveted program for morons? I believe it is simply because the idea of a job is so deeply rooted in the consciousness of most Typicals that they no longer question it. No matter how it was originally conceived, perhaps as a humane alternative to filling the hours of retarded people, it misses the meaning of an individual, assigning them to roles they can only fill analogically as dancing bears. While I decry vocational programs, I am not above using them for our purposes.

Langdon University has co-opted the charter school to legitimize our existence as an educational program; likewise, to legitimize our vocational program, we file the necessary paperwork to comply with the regulations of the states surrounding the university, and we institute a vocational program of Attilians hired by the university to act as teacher aids for programs serving Mongoloids. This service is funded by our donor and welcomed by most outside programs and organizations. These teacher aides, however, are effectively traveling subversive missionaries, much like Mormons, who infiltrate various programs for our kind.

43

Water

Amy and Charles have been collaborating, hatching a plan every bit as subversive as our missionary program, one that will move Langdon University and its mission to a new level. They come to me with their new idea. "We want to buy a water company," Charles explains. "Water makes sense on a number of fronts. Filtered water would give us a delivery system for getting gene therapy to Standards in their institutional environments while protecting Typicals from its effects."

"Also, we have identified water as the most valuable resource in the world, exceeding even that of oil," says Amy, taking up the narrative. "It's a good investment, and we can staff the company with Attilians through our vocational program without raising undue scrutiny."

Charles continues with the proposal: "We have found a water filtering company called Rita that makes household carafes to filter tapwater with disposable filters. It's currently valued at $400 million. Even if it were for sale, we are not yet in a position to purchase the company outright, but we'll engage in a program of accumulating a significant amount of stock so we can become a force in the company. Rita does not produce all of its disposable filters but supplements their own production by contracting with other companies to produce them. We have found a small plant that makes water filters for Rita that we can acquire for less than $5 million. This, in and of itself, may seem an ancillary product, but it's critical to our plan."

Amy who has been looking on, then delivers the *coup de grace*. "I've recently been engaged in a drug development program," she states. "My group and I have synthesized a compound that mimics the effects of cocaine without the addictive qualities—it is actually closer to a vitamin than a drug. It is suspected that this additive, introduced into the water via the water filter, will confer the same advantage that cocaine bestowed on earlier formulas of Coca-Cola. We anticipate it will increase sales of the treated filters significantly." They both settle into silence and look at me expectantly. I've never been a fan of the term *nonplussed*, but I stand there looking back at them nonplussed. I'm not sure why they have approached me before the others, but I'm honored.

"I think it's a hell of an idea" is all I can think to say.

We put Matthew out front as the public face in our corporate interactions. His lack of dominant Mongoloid features (Attila at best could only be his grandfather) is a definite bonus. Matthew enters into negotiations with Pine Tree Filtration Systems out of Portland, Maine, and we buy it for $4.75 million. Pine Tree produces filters for Rita water carafes in the area of New England and around the Northeast coast, and represents about ten percent of Rita's filters.

With the acquisition of Pine Tree, we begin lacing the filters with our Coke-like additive. An advantage to our plans is that Amy's compound needs only to be administered in small doses. Once we have added our Mongoloid work force to the company, it takes two visits to the plant by Amy and her crew to make the modifications to the filter fabrication procedures, and these are maintained by personnel of the university's vocational program. We buy a small apartment complex to house our workers and meet the paperwork requirements and regulations of Maine for residential programs for special-needs individuals—aka, tards, feebs, and morons.

After a short latency period, sales of Rita systems in New England and the Northeastern coast soar dramatically in unprecedented numbers. We barely manage to buy ten percent of Rita stock, but the success of the New England and Northeast coast sales increase the worth of our stock, and we use these dividends to buy more stock. The unprecedented gains are not duplicated in any other part of the Rita territories.

As our coffers begin to fill, we don't extend our program to other geographic areas, since our efforts would increase the worth of the company, thereby increasing the potential price of the company that we want to buy. With more entrepreneurial activities and the success of the old strategies we continue to extend our wealth. While Logan's selling-short program is still our biggest cash cow, the rising tide of our water holdings are a close second.

Within six months, Matthew executes an offer and the Rita governing board accepts it. Matthew demonstrates his developing business acumen by keeping the entire governing board as well as the CEO in place after we purchase the company. Water will occupy a pride of place in our future. We then move to acquire other companies producing water filters for Rita and bring the production completely in-house. We are then able to infiltrate the other filter providers, about half are produced by Rita itself, where we can add our Coke-like chemical.

The success of our chemical additive spawns a number of new products, travel water bottles, with new filter components produced by the company, filtration systems for office water coolers. As filters are replaced on a more frequent time schedule, people seem happier. This comes from reports of office productivity from those using the Rita water cooler system.

44

Reading Between the Letters

With our programs expanded to cover our teacher aides along with the workers at the Rita and other water filter plants, we needed a system to communicate with them. The most subversive of our activities is the treatment of Standard Mongoloids with the aqueous gene therapy treatment. The delivery system proved relatively easy to pull off, but our burgeoning program of providing teacher aides to organizations serving Mongoloids posed a greater challenge. With the subversive educational programs of instruction and methods, the importance of maintaining secrecy became a paramount challenge.

Our teacher aides are primarily transformed Mongoloids, with just a few Typicals providing cover; as such, these aides are not generally put into teaching positions. But one enticement to the cooperating organizations is to provide them with top-of-the-line computers. Included with these donations is a cadre of trained Mongoloid computer aides. In all but a few cases, the level of our people's expertise is far greater than that of the Typicals in charge. Typicals, for the most part, are content to let our aides provide the lion's share of the computer instruction; thus, there is little opposition by Typical workers to letting the aides take over a role that normally would be conducted by them. This system allows for our people to spend significant time with the otherwise captives of these institutions.

We were providing so many computers to these organizations that we decided to purchase a small computer company. Our technical people, from our cellphone enterprise (more on this in a minute), redesigned them and developed a superior product, including a language program developed by our resident linguist, Holly. This provided for communication between Langdon and the missionaries in the field. We labeled this system Reading Between the Letters.

The program uses the shape of the spaces between letters of written texts to represent words and phrases signaling the reader to move back and forth between parts of the text. Holly's study of written Oriental languages was her inspiration. The system is eidetic rather than phonetic, apologies to the monkey. It's efficient since a number of the space shapes exist as word combinations and even short phrases that are combined into a single shape. I think of how much fun it would be to instruct the deceased Ted, Holly's and my first teacher, in the use of her new reading method. I feel a twinge of regret at the thought.

Another advantage of the compact script is that we have placed our text into words that become the text of children's books, which we in turn publish and donate to our infiltrated programs. These books are age-appropriate for two- to eight-year-olds, analogous to the *Policeman is Your Friend*, and cover topics such as self-help, survival skills, counting and primary arithmetic, and Holly's favorite, animal alphabet books. A variety of story books, modeled after books like *Where the Wild Things Are*, are all vessels used to contain our surreptitious messages, and instructional material to our members and new students. The system has been translated into over 60 languages globally, from French to Telugu.

We developed a publishing company to meet our ever-increasing demand. The books have even been picked up by Typical parents for their children. By these means, we keep in touch with all of our Attilians, educate our new members, plan new projects, and keep our secrets.

If this book is ever published, it will carry a title like *Little Bear Joins the Fire Department*. Look for it at your local bookstore.

Phase V

Stepping out

45

The Letter is an L

Holly and I have had a bond ever since I cheated off her early letter recognition exercises with Ted. In fact, my early education was driven primarily by my need to show off for her. Since that time, we have sought each other's company during social group meetings and in our time at the university, but we have never seen each other outside of these situations. As we begin to step out beyond the confines of school and even the university, I become aware that all of my knowledge is artificial, buffered by books and the internet, and only my experience of being a Mongoloid is authentic knowledge. I go places with my mother and father, and on our various field trips, but I have limited independent social interaction with the world at large. My first forays into the Typical social landscape were not great successes, the aborted attempt at enrolling in a Typical cooking class, and the disaster represented by my calculus experiment. Still, my early defeats seem a poor reason not to try again. And Holly is my goal.

In the past year, I had read literally hundreds of books with romantic themes. From *Lady Chatterley's Lover*, to some in sleazier genres with titles like *Rebecca and Desire*. While I modestly counted myself among the world's most intelligent people as a 15-year-old, I harbored the same emotions as my Typical peers. I think I loved Holly from the first time I saw her. And I think she also feels affection for me. So, time to step out and fess up.

I confess that this new intrepid approach scares me. "Scares the shit out of me," as Logan would describe it. I'm way better at manipulating facts and information than my mother, but she is way better at manipulating society and culture. I ask her for advice. "Mom, what do you do when you're in love?

"Mason, are you in in love?" she responds quizzically, not completely able to stifle a chuckle.

"Yes, I think I am," I say, feeling incredibly awkward and vulnerable. I continue stiffly, "I need to know how to proceed."

"I take it this is with a girl." She's still smiling.

"Yes, Holly."

"Oh, she's very pretty."

"Mom, why is the first thing people say about a girl or woman is whether she's pretty?" This remark seems to chasten her, and she swallows her impending chuckle.

"Point taken, Mason," she says, accepting the question as an implicit criticism. "I've also been taken by Holly; her intelligence and civility are certainly more important than her looks."

I'm beginning to regret my remark. "It's OK, Mom. But what do I do?" I persist.

"Well, I'm hardly a player, I've not had a lot of experience myself," she says, and her uncharacteristic giggle is back. "But I think I'd start by asking her out on a date."

I'm familiar with the word but have no actual experience with it. "A date?" I echo.

"Yes, just the two of you, go out together and do something. See a movie, go to a museum, go out to dinner. It's difficult to get to know someone, really know them, around a lot of people. I think the purpose of dating is to have mutual experiences just between two people. A date could give you and Holly the experience of being together, just the two of you."

I take in her words, review my history of romantic literature, or at least romantic writing, and smile. "Mom, that's genius." Now it's my turn to giggle.

Armed with a plan, I confront Holly the next day at the university. "Holly..." We're standing in the kitchen, indulging in Irene's tea and sugar cookies. "Holly, you know it's difficult to know someone, really know someone when you're around a lot of people." She looks at me wonderingly.

"Mason, what are you talking about?" I remember how I felt the first time I sat next to her, being tested on the letters of the alphabet by Ted, how I felt the closeness between us, how my heart jumped, or however I described it at the time. I experience the same feelings now. Despite the growth of 150 IQ points, my feelings are the same. So is my bumbling behavior.

Best to fess up. "I think we should go out on a date together." Then I add hastily, "Get to know each other as boyfriend and girlfriend." I add this from nowhere. My ears are throbbing, my face is hot and probably as red as a DC fire truck.

I'm grateful that she does not laugh but looks at me earnestly and smiles.

"I think that's a very good idea." The whole of the kitchen is now the color of her golden hair, surrounding her in a corona. "Where do you think we should go?" she asks, returning the kitchen to its normal colors. And I can breathe again, restoring oxygen to my deprived brain.

I'd been giving that some thought. "Ice skating," I reply. I had just read a young adult novel, not great literature but appealing to my incipient romanticism, about a boy and a girl in Holland who come together while ice skating on frozen Dutch rivers. I had conjured images of Holly and me ice skating. It wouldn't be on frozen rivers, but it wasn't a movie, ether.

"Brilliant," she says, and she jumps up and down a few times and claps. I mumble a few words softly to myself, but Holly hears. "What did you say?" she asks, attentively.

"The letter is an L," I answer self-consciously.

"Why did you say that?"

"It was the first letter that Ted asked me that I didn't know, that first day we were together at the clinic. I didn't know it when I sat down, but I stole it from your answer. 'The letter is an L.' It's when I fell in love with you."

46

Obe

We set our date for the upcoming Saturday. There were two issues to resolve before our ice-skating adventure. As it turned out, Holly solved them both. The first was where to ice skate, since there were no frozen rivers nearby as we were in the middle of summer. I briefly entertained the idea going to Holland to complete my fantasy, but it was summer there, too, as well as being a bit impractical and premature. I say premature since it would be economically possible for us to go. We all had voted to provide each Attilian with an ample personal bank account that was increasing every day, though none of us so far had made much use of it.

I mention this problem to Holly, who says, "Why don't we go to the local ice skating rink?" Ice skating rink? In all my reading and net surfing, I was ignorant of anything to do with ice skating other than the romantic novel and was unaware of ice rinks. Holly explained ice rinks, and this seemed an easy fix to our problem. We looked up ice rinks near us and decided on one in Virginia nearby. The next problem was how we could get there. My mother would take us, but that would defeat our goal of just the two of us. "Taxi," said the worldly Holly, and she left me feeling like the idiot, marinating in what I still didn't know.

Saturday comes faster than it ever has before. Holly's mother delivers her to my mother's house, and we call a DC cab. My mother is as nervous as I am, making sure we have our cellphones and know the address of the ice rink. "Do you have enough money?" she asks.

"Yes, Mom, I have fifty dollars cash and Holly and I have debit cards with a hundred thousand dollars between us."

"Yes," she replies awkwardly, "I know." My mother still is having trouble getting used to my financial independence.

The taxi comes driven by a very dark black man who gets out of the car and waits for us.

"Do you want me to tell him where you're going?" asks my mother, unable to keep interjecting herself.

"I think we can handle that, Ms. Free," Holly answers diplomatically.

"Of course." My mother's hand reaches up and grabs her throat.

"We better get out of here quick before she has a meltdown," I whisper to Holly as we walk to the waiting cab. The driver opens the back door, and we both get in. However, he leaves the door open and waits.

There's a period of awkward silence. "Is your mother coming?" he asks with heavily accented English.

"No," I say.

"Oh, it's just the two of you, very, very good. Where you two goin'?" Holly tells him our destination.

"Where are you from?" asks the social Holly.

"Togo. You know where it is?"

"Yes, West Africa, but don't you speak French?"

"Oui, Mademoiselle, but I come to America and I have to learn English, such as it is." All of this is in French.

Holly answers him in impeccable French. "Have you seen any elephants?"

"Oh, yes, my cousin is a game warden in Nigeria. I have seen many elephants." He has returned to his accented English to include me in the conversation.

"I love elephants."

"Me too, young Miss."

"My name is Holly."

"It's a pleasure indeed, Miss Holly. My name is Obe. I have a longer African name, but it is hard to say. Obe is better."

"What's your African name?" I ask, breaking into the conversation.

Laughing, he replies, "Oberjukendokeiwingo. Can you say it?"

I repeat it back to him. "Very, very good, you are the first American to do it. Even my family can't do it, only my mother, she's the one who gave it to me. It's a number of words strung together."

The cab has stopped in front of Wonder Ice. I pay the fifteen-dollar cab fee along with a twenty percent tip. "You gave me three dollars too much, young sir," says Obe.

"Twenty percent tip. Mason," I say and hold out my hand.

Obe takes it, then reaches into his shirt pocket and pulls out a card. "Call the number and I'll come back and pick you up."

"What if you're driving someone else?" asks Holly, ever practical.

"Don't worry, Miss Holly. I'll be free."

47

The Ice Rink

As we walk into the cool breath of the ice rink, illuminated by a surfeit of varied neon lights. I reach down and take Holly's hand. It is meant to be an intimate gesture; it would not be the last hand holding of the day. We walk to the counter where we get our skates and pay for the skating. The guy at the counter is a middle-aged, balding, fat guy who only ice skates in his dreams. He looks hard at the two of us and says, "I don't know. Are your parents with you? I'm not sure I can rent you these skates," and I'm back in Vice principal Meanan's office.

But over the last year I've lost a good deal of my patience with prejudice. "Call the fuckin' manager."

He looks at me like I just stepped on his foot with an ice skate. "What do you think, Rick?" he says to his partner at the counter.

"Give him the skates, Jake, or go call Scanlen." We give Jake our shoe sizes, and he gives us our skates, with the instruction to "be safe." It is here that I begin to rethink my romantic notions of ice skating. First, as I lace up my skates, I see there is a 35-centimeter steel blade running the length of the boot, and less than a half centimeter in width. I knew you skated on blades but never paused to think about what it would take to stand on one, much less two, on a surface with minimal traction. I make my way out onto the rink, walking on the sides of my feet. Holly, as it turns out, was born in Flint, Michigan, and has been on ice skates since she was four. We get on the ice, and the first thing I do is the splits, winding up on my ass looking up at Holly from the frozen floor, as the ice rink is suddenly filled with Johann Strauss music that soars over the PA system.

Worse, I try to stand back up but can get no purchase on the ice as my blades slide ineffectually on the frozen surface. I walk on my knees to the short wooden wall that defines the limits of the rink and drag myself up, where I stand with collapsed ankles, the blade of my skate on one side of my foot, the edge of my instep on the other.

Romance has ceded to ignominy, and Holly, assessing the situation, takes my hands and pulls me forward while skating backward. "Try to stand up on your skates. You slide better that way," is her soft instruction. This I do for about thirty seconds before my ankles buckle and I pitch headlong onto the ice, dragging Holly down with me. I'm mortified. Holly, however, is laughing. There's lots of hand holding and hugging but not the kind I was longing for. Rather, I'm involved in a Mongolian clusterfuck, to use one of Logan's favorite images. *A Mongoloid clusterfuck*, I think sardonically.

With all my physical and technical limitations, we manage to put in a respectable ninety minutes on the ice. I spend a good half of the time in a prone position. By the end, with Holly's aid and instruction, I can skate short distances on my own. Repeatedly, I proudly skate a few feet next to Holly, then in midsentence hit the deck while watching her slide away from me into the distance.

Jake smirks as we return our skates. "I see you made it," he says sarcastically, observing the little bit of blood in my nose.

"Yes, we did very well," Holly offers, looking at me and smiling. I remain silent.

We retrieve our shoes from the locker. Holly takes out a Kleenex and a bottle of water from her small backpack and cleans the blood off my nose. "I think you were very brave," she says. And with that all the earlier disgrace evaporates. I only realize later all of the bonding that occurred during the ill-conceived first attempt at stepping out.

"What next?" I ask, my fragile ego boosted by Holly's comment.

"Let's eat." We exit the skating rink and go looking for a restaurant.

"Should I call Obe?"

"Not yet, let's walk."

"Fine with me." I reach out and hold her hand. We get a lot of looks from passersby, many of whom smile at us and look just a little too long. I'm bothered by it, but Holly smiles back with a hi or hello. "Don't these looks and smiles bother you?" I ask her.

"No. You shouldn't be bothered by sweetness, or by curiosity."

"I guess," I say truculently, but upon later reflection I would see the wisdom of her words; they would become important to our stepping out.

We walk a long way into a neighborhood with which we are both unfamiliar. Obe would tell us that it was a section called Adams Morgan. It was full of shops and restaurants from all over the world. "Let's have Indian food," says Holly. She's excited, and we choose a restaurant called Joyti, which Holly tells me means fire in Hindi. Holly is an accomplished linguist. "I'm enamored of languages and the geography, and cultures that go with them," she explains.

"That's how you spoke French to Obe?" I ask.

"Yes. I spend most of my time on the Internet studying languages, finding out about the people who speak them, where and how they live. Someday I want to travel." She smiles shyly as if she might have divulged too much. I, on the other hand, am thrilled with her sharing.

"I would like to travel," I say as we walk into Joyti.

A jovial waiter installs us at a table near the street, looks around, and asks if others are coming, looking surprised when we say no. This was a common reaction we would encounter frequently in our stepping out—an assumption that we could not be out on our own. The waiter, Rahul, is polite and tries not to show his surprise as he takes our order. Holly is not only fluent in Hindi but has an awareness of Indian fare. Despite the fact that she has never had any authentic Indian food, she orders for us and says a few words of Hindi in doing so. The waiter looked as though the vase of flowers on the table has spoken. He was impressed even though he said he was Punjabi and Hindi was not his native language. Holly was embarrassed with what she felt was her cultural *faux pas*. She would go home and learn to speak Punjabi within the week. "It has some similarity to Hindi," she would say, "though the alphabet is different."

Holly is familiar with the names of dishes, but not the amount, and we are served with enough food for ten people. As at the ice rink, we comport ourselves respectably, and easily eat enough for four people. Still, we leave with a large bag filled with to-go boxes.

We exit the restaurant into the street lined with small shops painted in bold colors, exuding exotic smells and expelling unfamiliar music. People speak many different languages that Holly does her best to identify. We browse a few shops, and I buy Holly a bronze pendant of the elephant-headed Hindu god, Ganesha. When I buy a gold chain to accompany it, I use my debit card. The clerk looks suspiciously at me and shows surprise when the card goes through. However, I'm getting used to the scrutiny and becoming less annoyed by it. Holly is ecstatic with the gift.

The sun is going down when we call Obe, who answers on the second ring. We give him the address and he is delighted that we had found Adams Morgan. "Adams Morgan, very very good." Within ten minutes, we are sitting in his cab.

We stop at Holly's house first, and Obe gets out of the cab and opens the door. "Goodbye, Miss Holly." Then he adds, "You two are not what you seem. If you ever need a taxi, please call me." I walk Holly to her door, and at the step she turns and kisses me—my heart sings.

At my mom's house, Obe does not open the door but turns around and says, "See you later, Mason. I own my own cab, so it is always with me. Call me anytime." We shake hands.

A very, very good day, my first kiss and our first outside friend.

My mother waits expectantly at the door. "Well, how was it?" she says, trying not to show her anticipation.

"I was very brave."

48

The Mongoloid Expert

Other than social milestones, our first venture outside called further attention to the inferiority of knowledge gained through simulated formats such as books and the Internet. These sources are good for substantiating and reinforcing experiences but don't substitute for them. Holly and I discuss the topic back at Langdon and conclude that it is vital for Attilians to continue to expand their interactions with Typical society. This process was first started with the young people employed at the Rita water filtering plant in Portland, Maine, then extended to the workers in the newly acquired companies, who are the vanguard of this movement—those living and working independently making inroads in their respective communities.

What we learn from Obe, and even the Indian waiter, Rahul, is that you can dramatically alter attitudes in a very short time with small displays of competence. We acknowledge that these are small steps, but important to pointing the way in the future.

All the Attilians have their areas of expertise. Charles is our expert on IT; Logan is an expert in financial matters; Andrew is a hedge fund whiz; Amy is our leader in biochemistry and genetics; Polly, our psychologist; Susan, our lawyer; and June is our assassin. Although not always followed, Holly is our moral compass. My expertise, however, is Mongoloids. As my consciousness expanded, I had become intrigued with what it means to be Mongoloid. From my earliest research foray into Mongolians to my experiment with calculus, I was the one paying close attention to our biological and social conditions. My penchant for using politically incorrect language is an active, albeit cynical heuristic warning against mitigating our position in history. Stepping out was just the newest frontier.

Earlier, I wrote a pamphlet on how to avoid unwanted scrutiny of our emerging intellect and knowledge. *Rules for Being Mongoloid* described methods to simulate the behavior and appearance of Standards, to not call undue attention to ourselves. A feeling of vulnerability fostered this need for secrecy. After Holly's and my date, I begin to think that maybe this tactic was a bit excessive, perhaps a little overly defensive and restrictive. Leaving this part of our history behind, which is certainly where history belongs, Holly and I agree that we should step cautiously out into society and become more visible. We decide to engage in a stepping out program and develop policies and suggestions on how to engage in it, with the goal of writing something like a handbook for other Attilians. We have been encouraged by the results of our fessing-up campaign and have gained strength from our parents' positive reactions to our new abilities.

We take our recent experiences with Obe, Jake at the ice rink, Rahul the Indian waiter, the shopkeeper's scrutiny my use of a debit card, and the probing and curious looks from people on the street, and we develop a program with guidelines for others to access the community at large. Holly and I are surprised that the group is split down the middle. Some, like Logan, welcome the approach. "Fucking A, let's get out of our shit box," he says. Others, like John and June, are hostile and distrust the approach, expressing a deep prejudice of Typicals and their society. June: "We can never trust them." John: "If we let them into our lives they will destroy us, hold us captive to their prejudice." Holly and I argue that as we became more involved in the world, we should know how to function within it. The opponents argue that we are better off if we keep the Typicals and their society at a distance, since they would never be willing partners. At one point in his opposition, Charles paraphrases Thomas Edison's comment about mathematicians when he says, "When I need a Typical I'll hire one."

At one point in our meeting, Susan calls for a vote, and Holly and I are given the go-ahead by a 9-to-7 majority. Hardly the ringing endorsement we had expected. We are free to go on with our plan, but the vote highlights deep divisions within our group.

49

Recommendations for Stepping Out

Deep divisions aside, Holly and I begin our research. Aiding in the process is Obe, who has taken an interest in both of us and always seems to be available. We go to the National Zoo so Holly can see "real live" elephants, and Obe joins us. The trip is a mixed success as Holly is appalled at some of the environments in which the animals are kept. She loves the elephants, though her parting comment is, "I don't think I like zoos. The animals should be in their native habitats." I think of telling her that their native habitats are being destroyed at an appalling rate. But I know her well enough to keep quiet.

She has conversations with Obe, who has a lot of information about elephants. Holly shows elation at every new bit of information or story. However, we both notice that when Obe is with us, our interactions with Typicals are radically diminished as people tended to think Obe is in charge of us, directing questions or comments to him rather than to us. The solicitous smiles abound. This leads us to write: "On your excursions into the community, don't go with a Typical if you want to establish contact or alter perceptions." We decide to take Obe along only when we wanted to socialize with him. This does not seem to discourage him, as he maintains a distance surreptitiously behind. He's so adroit and unobtrusive that we don't mind.

Other principles:

> • *Go back to people and places that you frequented before, even if the first try wasn't a success. Some people don't catch on with one trial.*
>
> • *Develop long-term relationships, and friendships where it is appropriate.*

Holly and I had returned to the Indian restaurant, Joyti, a number of times, speaking to the waiter Rahul in his native Punjabi. Holly took the lead, but I manage to stumble along behind. Rahul is always excited and treats us like VIP patrons.

> • *Don't be bumptious or irritated by Typical's initial reactions. Give them time to process the situation. It's as new to them as it is to us. If you come to an impasse, just walk away and try again later, or try another place.*

While this was patently not my strategy with Jake at the ice rink, it proved to be a good tactic in other interactions.

> • *Be confident in your interactions or requests. Demonstrate a knowledge beyond the scope of your immediate interaction or request, but don't appear to be superior.*
>
> • *Frequent locally owned businesses over large stores or operations. Person-to-person relationships are easier to modify than are corporate bureaucratic and impersonal policies.*
>
> • *Foreigners are often more receptive than members of our own ethnic group. Give white people more chances and time, for some reason they seem to be more tied to their social biases.*

• When engaging in a social interaction, start slowly and take your cues from those with whom you are interacting. Don't be initially upset with condescension. This will disappear as you demonstrate competence and develop a relationship.

• Use your debit card where you can, as it provides a certain status. Don't be perturbed when more identification is requested. Tip liberally, at least 20% in restaurants, more if the service is good, but don't over-do it.

50

The Accounting

Langdon University functions more like a think tank than an institution of higher education. We comprise small groups that engage in particular areas of research and projects, often operating independently from the larger group. We then meet in a forum and engage in what we call an "accounting," where small groups account for themselves, share their findings, and propose new projects or directions. This system works well at keeping everyone appraised, connected, and informed with all the necessary information we need to make group decisions. In addition, this structure provides the freedom to pursue the interests of individuals without being hampered by the cautions of others.

We would typically call for an accounting about once a month. Holly and I thought to update the group after about two months of our stepping out. In addition to our recommendations, we compiled a list of the different activities, destinations, and outcomes that we had experienced. Our presentation takes place in the middle of the meeting. Everything has been perfunctory to that point, and we start with our list. In the beginning, most people smile and nod, often injecting the results of outings of their own. Before we can move on to the principles derived from our experience, a few in the group voice hostile or negative reactions from their own experiences in the community, primarily dealing with condescension or not being allowed to complete their desired interactions. Holly and I recount similar experiences and their resolution. However, the hostility is directed not at the experience itself but at the idea of stepping out in the first place. While not being the majority view, it is enough of the group to cause concern. The chief criticism is that we are accommodating to a system of inferiors. This is the first time Typicals are actively called inferior, though it has been implied many times.

The most vocal and adamant proponent of this view is Charles, our original leader. Charles relates a story about a time he was denied entry into a taxi, the driver not accepting that he could be on his own. Charles is livid as he recounts the event. I ask if he had tried again. Charles states that he had taken the next taxi in the queue. I said that this is standard; when you get refused, you try again and it usually works out.

"Well, I'm not the expert," he says sarcastically, "but that's really not the point."

"What is the point?" I ask. Charles looked daggers at me. Holly reaches over and takes my hand.

"The point is that these people are inferior to us, yet they exert power on the basis of their bias," he retorts. I could see a good number of our group nodding. Our group is now about ninety.

"But that is just the point," I respond, "we're engaged in combatting bias. We're attempting to change attitudes." More heads are shaking now than nodding in support of my words.

Charles continues, "I'm not interested in changing attitudes, I'm interested in changing the population."

I can see no profit in continuing the debate. "I think we need to establish a working group on stepping out," I say, to end the discussion. The group is obviously agitated, and further accounting is postponed for another time.

Holly and I are upset by the rancor directed at Typicals and their society. This is partially mitigated by those who come up to us after the meeting to sign on to our working group. But we are obviously dealing with a good deal of anger and bias within our own group.

51

Daniel

aniel is a quiet and unassuming boy who was part of the original gene therapy group, and as such he's one of the elite fifteen, elite sixteen with Matthew. No one had taken much notice of Daniel in the past, and he seemed content with his position in the group. I had tried to involve him in conversations a few times but found him taciturn and reticent to engage, so I stopped trying. Daniel seemed fine with his situation, so I left it alone. However, I was surprised at our next accounting when he spoke up. "I have something I'd like to share." he ventures, when Amy and her group finish their presentation. Daniel had vaguely attached himself to Amy's group but was not a dominant member. I'm not the only one who shows surprise when he speaks without preamble and states, "I make explosives."

52

The Hidin' It Days Are Over

One byproduct of the stepping-out program is that there seems an unlimited reserve of Typicals who, with little hesitation or reluctance, adjust seamlessly to our new social roles and abilities. Holly and I have found this to be true, but it is also substantiated by the experiences of others. This is to the chagrin of Charles and the isolationists in our group, who treat these anecdotes with skepticism and derision. "These are just perturbations, freak examples from an otherwise biased and complicit population" is just one of Charles' scathing assessments of positive stepping-out anecdotes. Others echo similar sentiments.

Despite our internal divisions and the bellicose rhetoric applied to them, the stepping-out experiences provide a pool of copasetic and willing Typicals who can be deployed to act as our agents in society at large. Even Charles and his like-minded colleagues have had to acknowledge their benefit. Matthew has been our non-Mongoloid face to society, but he is becoming increasingly stretched. We have become too big.

It has been three years since the founding of Langdon University and three and a half since the start of the gene therapy program. Rita, our water program, is now in five states and staffed by a thousand tards, who are also involved routinely with engaging Typical allies. Logan's Fuck-it app still has a consistent following but nowhere near its initial frenzy. Selling-short remains our cash cow, followed by water, but a new program threatens to eclipse them both. Charles, John, and the IT group have spent their time developing a new cellphone system that rivals existing providers. The handset itself is superior to others, by virtue of being waterproof, and is nearly indestructible, and has an operating system that is easier to use than its competitors. Charles quips that a major factor guiding development is the stupidity native to Typicals. "It has to be easy since they're so dumb." A prototype is developed and distributed to group members. Charles, though an isolationist, increasingly talks of enlisting the aid of Typicals in furthering this enterprise.

Our outreach to educational and welfare agencies serving Mongoloids is in full swing and stretching our resources to keep up with it. In these programs, Standards are treated with a gene therapy mixture dissolved in our Rita water that is made available in all of the organizations. Amy continues to improve the therapeutic and delivery system. With all our new recruits, it is becoming increasingly more difficult to keep a lid on our abilities. We have already had several inquiries from the press and later from the professional rehabilitation community for information on our curious status. Something had to be done to legitimize our increasing participation in society at large.

I scour the professional journals, both psychology and special education, and feel the psychological journals are not as political as the special education ones. We have a history of being confronted with the benevolent biases of the special education and rehabilitation community. The psychology journals are colder but less emotionally prone to be political. Still, they have their own axes to grind.

I write an article, published in the *Journal of Clinical Psychology*, defining a new syndrome that combines Down Syndrome with aspects of Asperger's syndrome, a high-functioning form of autism, in which affected persons demonstrate forms of genius abilities in areas such as mathematics, science, music, and memory. I describe a number of case studies of our people done under controlled conditions. The article is meant to provide us with some cover and to blunt the requests for more information. Like my calculus experiment, this is a naive miscalculation! Rather than quelling the requests for interviews, we become deluged with them, as well as inquiries from interested parents. The reaction from the professional community is generally hostile, and the article is primarily met with disbelief.

My mother had warned me of the danger of involving the professional community that tended to be conservative even when, like at present, it advocated for more participation and inclusion, their views tended to be politically biased, inflexible, and doctrinaire. While I listened to her closely, she had no alternative and, in the end, reminiscent of calculus, I imprudently forged ahead.

As Logan put it, "The shit has really hit the fan on this one—the hidin' it days are over, dude." As indeed they were. The criticisms came from a number of professional directions. Most directly, the professionals wanted to know who was I and what my credentials were. I hadn't signed my name, that would have been folly, but published it on behalf of the Langdon University Genetics Group. Their next question was, "What in the hell is Langdon University?" The answer is not impressive. A charter school for morons and feebs carries little weight. Had Dr. Malone not been in a comatose state, all of his earlier protests would have been confirmed, but he'd jumped the gun.

We had a few supporters, though. The journal had accepted the article based primarily upon the quality of the case studies, and initially supported us as mostly a reflex against the criticism and outrage. Which notably came from special education and rehab groups serving people with Down Syndrome, who felt this was prank.

53

Focused Down Syndrome

My mother once again comes to the rescue and hooked us up with a researcher, a willing Typical, from the National Institute of Mental Health. I still don't know how she went about recruiting her.

A note here: My mother was aware of her status as a non-professional occupying the position of the director of the Office of Special Education, and she surrounded herself with qualified personnel from a variety of fields; she never thought that she was smarter than anyone else, and she deferred to the experience and expertise of others. It is surprising how few leaders follow this approach. In doing so, my mother always had people she could rely on when the need arose. Dr. Hanna Bartell was only the most recent. My mother asked only one thing from me, and it was a big ask. She said I needed to come clean with Dr. Bartell so that she could know what the implications of her research and writing might be, and not get out over her skies, the term she used. My mother was learning to live with a certain amount of deception, but she was always fair. She arranges a meeting with Dr. Bartell and me that takes place in her office.

"I hear you've gotten yourself into an interesting position," Dr. Bartell says with understatement.

"Yes," I say, not knowing how to begin. "I'm a genius. Or at least a genius by the standards of Typical society," I correct. *Fucking lame*, I think as I retreat into Loganese.

"Typical?" she probes.

"It's what we call non-Mong- … non-Down Syndrome people."

"I've read the term but never heard it used."

"Yeah, we didn't invent it, I only co-opted it. But it's a good description, don't you think?"

"Yes, I do. I think a lot of our thinking and indeed science can be described by the term and the somewhat derogatory way I think you mean it. Tell me how you arrived at this point," she says, looking directly at me. I feel I'm being dissected, and shiver.

"My friends and I were part of a gene replacement therapy program to make us smarter, and it made us smarter than almost everyone," I continue in my lameness.

"But that's a good thing, isn't it?"

"It is and it isn't," I reply. "If Typical society knew about us, they would put an end to us, at least us as a growing movement. They would certainly end the program that we are promoting to transform every Mong- … Down Syndrome person we can reach. There's a split in our ranks. Some feel we should engage with Typicals, others feel we should keep ourselves to ourselves, strictly secret. I'm with the majority and think we should interact more with Typicals and Typical society, but to do that we needed a cover to explain some of our actions. I thought if I could define a new syndrome that would explain some of our higher-functioning behavior, it would give us that cover. But it only seems to have aroused suspicion, scrutiny, and hostility." *And it's not the first time*, I remind myself.

Hanna Bartell looks at me a very long time, then says, "I'm going to help you, Mason, you and your colleagues, but you'll have to help me. Do I have your word that you'll help me and not hold back any relevant information that I would need to know?" I assure her that I will. Though I know she has many other questions, she stands up, shakes my hand, and leaves me in my mother's office with questions of my own.

No matter what concerns she may have entertained, this willing partner constructs a protocol to test my assertions. The hidin' it days are nearly over. In order to reveal as little about ourselves as is possible, we assemble a group of thirty modified Mongoloids that will be put through the NIMH protocol. This seems to be a sufficient number to substantiate the claims put forward in my article. Only a few of the thirty are original members of the gene therapy group, but it is easy since we now have literally thousands to choose from. Hanna designs an experiment that will address one or two particular abilities rather than a general competence across the board to mimic the Asperger's form of autism. If we can get through this, we have the possibility to mitigate the effects of scrutiny from Typical professionals and their organizations. One unexpected source of support comes from Charles, who says that the overall effect from this might be positive, and he volunteers to be one of the subjects of the protocol. Another subject is me.

The results of the new research, conducted by our conscript, corroborates my initial claims and elaborates them. Dr. Bartell quickly authors a journal article that helps to substantiate the original assertions and takes the heat off us by garnering more credibility in the medical-psychological-educational community. Hanna Bartell also goes on to conduct further studies that bring Focused Down Syndrome, her original term, to a reputable place in the professional literature. For these studies, Hanna uses Standards—her research highlighting certain iconoclastic abilities of non-transformed Mongoloids; freeing herself and Focused Down Syndrome from overt duplicity.

54

Some Questions Answered

Although my mother is aware of her limitations in her current field, my father, on the other hand, has always considered himself as the smartest kid in the class, whatever that class was. I loved him, but this drove me crazy. Even when he realized that I was intellectually more varied and proficient then he was, he would seize upon opportunities to correct me with an understated and casual superiority that had become his defining persona. Usually it concerned a word or phrasing that he felt more precisely expressed what I had to say. Mostly I would let this go and either acquiesce to his suggestion or let it ride. In the case of phrasing, I would sometimes point out the author from whom I appropriated the phrase saying, "That's from Faulkner's *The Sound and the Fury*," or "it comes from Hemingway's *Fiesta*," and I would repeat from the original.

"*Fiesta?*" he said, hoping to catch me in an error.

"Sorry Dad," I'd said. "I read it in German, the English title is *The Sun Also Rises*." When I did this, it was as close as he ever came to fucking losing his cool, to use a Logan phrase. I didn't do it often, but when I did it felt good.

I once asked my mother how she came to be with him, as they seemed so different. "Is this the kind of question you ask when you get a girlfriend?" she responded jocularly to deflect it. I continued to stare. When she could see it was a serious inquiry, she assumed a faraway gaze, as if opening a door of her own.

"When I met your father, he was a young and frightened undergraduate, very bright, very sweet, and very unsure of himself. Given his lack of confidence, it was quite difficult for him to approach me; he did it so awkwardly and so sweetly, that he captured my heart. I know it's hard to believe today, but he was really quite vulnerable back then. I'll tell you a little story, I'm not even sure if it's accurate, but it's how I make sense of some things to myself.

"William belonged to a small fraternity, not one of the prominent houses, mostly peopled by academics. You know how your father loves baseball; the fraternity was in the process of fielding an intramural softball team, and I encouraged him to try out. He was hesitant but did it. It didn't go well, and I remember it was a tough time for him. He wasn't very good, and he was treated callously by the other team members. In the end, he didn't make the team; it was quite a blow, and he didn't take it at all well.

"First, he blamed me for encouraging him to try out, then he railed at the others for not seeing his talent, then he kind of closed up for a while. I told him that it was only a little team, what's the big deal, and other such things that only aggravated him. Eventually the sting seemed to fade and he returned to normal, but with a harder edge. This came at a time when he was experiencing academic success. He was writing and editing the campus newspaper with an occasional article in the local paper, letters to the editor and such. He began to realize the power of the written word and the power of his intellect, but again, the newfound prowess came with a hard edge.

"It seemed to me that it increasingly came to have a bullying quality— belittling people and ideas he didn't agree with. At the time, I attributed it to a flexing of new muscles. With me he was as sweet and gentle as he had always been and we married right after graduation. He took a job with the *Washington Post* that soon led to a position as an opinion writer and a syndicated columnist. He allied himself with conservative positions that I sometimes found heartless; when I confronted him, he would become hostile and dismissive. I didn't like many of our new friends whose ideas and fervor I didn't share." My mother looked off into the distance as if conjuring distasteful memories. "Some of those friendships, though, led directly to my appointment as an assistant secretary of education, where as it turns out, I've been quite useful." She smiles at me warmly, then returns her gaze to the horizon. "In the end, we just turned out to be people who, not without affection, shouldn't live together. Our take on the world was just too different."

I have a second question that I'm not so sure I want to know the answer to, but I ask it anyway. "Mom, when you and Dad were arguing about my participation in the gene therapy program, you said that he wasn't always satisfied with the way I was. What did you mean by that?"

"Oh dear, that was said in the heat of an intense argument, and it was not a completely fair statement. Your father always loved you from the time you were born, though neither of us knew much about how your condition would affect our lives. It was harder on him than it was on me, since care and programming for persons with Down Syndrome were forms of the social support system that your father advocated so strongly against. When he was confronted with it as an individual, he had to grapple with implications that were profoundly uncomfortable. He's never fully come to peace with it. Did you read the column he wrote about you, and what a great child you were, and how people needed to be more accepting?"

"Yes," I mumble.

"Well, that's about as close to a resolution as he got," she says. We have been in the car driving home from Landon, my mother's distant gaze has made me nervous at times, but by the time we pull into our garage, I have the answers I had asked for, and feel a new sympathy for my father. After that, I never again hit him with Faulkner or Hemingway.

55

Daniel and the Congressman

My mother proved herself to be an unflinching ally. We were all surprised when she, as assistant Secretary of Education and director of the Office of Special Education, became a target of a Congressman Cotton. Ely Cotton was a redneck former judge from South Carolina whose mission was to cut the funding of any and all federal social programs, and he was driven close to rabid by the Department of Education, probably because it taught people to read. He seized upon my mother and her shop as being the most vulnerable, along with the fact that my mother was a woman and a non-professional appointee, which to his downhome -eye looked like an easy target. Congress was filled at the time with like-minded yahoos, and Cotton marshalled a constituency against my mother, her programs, and the entitlements that secured the services. Not having any significant accomplishments over the past year and a half, Cotton and his cronies doubled down to pose a serious threat. We had a number of accountings that discussed the problem with lots of outrage but no substantial remedies. One suggestion came from Holly, who said, "Why don't we just vote him out?" We had just opened a Rita water filter plant in a small South Carolina town, which was staffed with over a thousand Attilian workers. We thought that this was an idea worth considering, as the population of Attilians now boasted hundreds of thousands of transformed Mongoloid souls. If we voted en masse, we could have a political influence greater than Ely Cotton.

Charles then spoke up. "If we did that it would completely blow our cover; we would not only become an intellectual threat, but a political one as well. What kind of retaliation would we incur from society? Better to keep working behind the scenes and maintain our secrecy."

Daniel, who had foreshadowed his upcoming explosive intervention, tells us his tale at the next accounting: "I kept a loose surveillance of Cotton through the Internet, and by hanging around the Capitol, and glimpsed him a few times. I was even allowed to observe his office—nobody pays any attention to a retard," he notes. "Fraid they might catch it. I just walked in and loitered, nobody protested. At the end of the day, I followed him to the garage where I identified his car. After that it was easy. I wired a small charge that I made and placed it on the underside of his car just below the driver's seat. I calculated the amount for a small charge enough to blow him up in his seat but not cause any other damage. I had it programmed to a cellphone, and I waited. I knew that there was to be a meeting at of the Confederate Flag Reinstatement Society slated for 3 p.m. in Fairfax. Sure enough, at 1:45 here he comes; gives me this great big toothy grin as he gets off the elevator and says, 'How, ya boy?' And I just smile.

"He gets into his car and I blow the charge when he's on the next level. The whole place is in upheaval, and I just walk away. I pass three or four guards who run right by me. Easy. He won't be bothering your mother anymore." He smiles at me.

There is some clapping at Daniel's news along with some head shaking. I confess to engaging in both. Holly is clearly on the head-shaking side. Sitting next to me, she grasps my slowly clapping hands and pulls them hard into her lap and whispers, "Our third murder."

Profile: Daniel

Daniel came to my mother's attention in the early stages of the funding process for the grant via an article in the *Washington Post*. The article described a situation where a young Mongoloid male was arrested along with gang members on drug and violence charges. The city, at the time, was in the midst of a crackdown on gang violence. The assistant district attorney in charge of the case was stymied that his prosecution of the young man named Daniel was not eligible due to his disability. The assistant DA was young and eager to make a name for himself. He initially refused to let the prosecution of Daniel drop, until a local disability rights group got involved and colloquially cleaned the young assistant DA's clock.

My mother was intrigued, and pursued the story, both out of an interest in the Down Syndrome youth and in response to a criticism from one of the grant reviewers who described the makeup of the study participants as too "pearly white". Daniel, a mixed-race child of a black father and white mother, lived in one of D.C.'s inner-city housing projects. My mother met with Daniel's mother, which resulted in adding a 15th participant to the protesting Dr. Malone's study. Just the first of a number of disagreements with the good doctor.

Although of mixed race, Daniel resembled his mother with respect to his complexion. This turned out to be important as it gave Daniel a certain anonymity in his movements among the outskirts of government and power. If his complexion gave him advantage in his chosen calling, it produced nothing but ridicule in his hood, making Daniel the target of much derision. This continued until the astute local gang leader found out that it was difficult to prosecute people with disabilities; from then on, Daniel had a home and a cadre of homies. His previously solitary existence was replaced by a place of honor, as he was routinely employed to transport guns and drugs with a virtual legal impunity to the gang's many clients. His complexion disappeared, and Daniel reveled in his new role, learning the ins and outs of juvenile delinquency. As Daniel's intellect progressed, so did his special brand of the antisocial, moving from transporting guns to a making sophisticated explosives, and conceiving creative ways to deploy them.

Along with Daniel's attraction to violence and his laser focus on his targets, he exhibited and maintained a personal morality that demanded no innocent beings be harmed in his explosions; this complicated the delivery but added a meticulous complexity to which Daniel always adhered.

From my initial revulsion of his acts, I came to admire Daniel and consider him one of my close friends. Indeed, his actions were as important to our movement as those of Charles, Amy, and Logan.

He writes:

> *"In my earliest memories of the neighborhood I grew up in, I have always hated injustice and hypocrisy—hypocrisy especially, particularly by those who have power over others. People who will say one thing to your face and do the opposite in their actions. The end never justifies the means— the ends justify themselves. If they don't—don't do them.*
>
> *"From my time working as a mule for the gang, I developed a distrust of people in power and society in general, those who buffer their acts with bureaucracy and mendacity. It is these people and their power I seek to destroy. I don't take these things on lightly, but I do take them personally— extremely personally. I make no excuses for my acts."*

56

Bastards

It's 5 o'clock now and we're ready to go home, but I pull out my laptop and find a shitload, a plethora, of articles describing the death of South Carolina Representative Ely Cotton, relating that he was killed in an explosion in his car on the way home from the House.

I read out a few of the articles to the group and there are some gasps. It is like no one fully believed Daniel's story until we received confirmation. When we all acknowledge its veracity, there continues to be a mixed reaction; there are cheers from a good number of members, not a few open mouths, and a few tears. Holly continues to look shocked, slowly shaking her head. John, however, cheers the loudest, "Yes," he says, "a new tool that we can use on the bastards." A number of low conversations circulate among members, as Harold comes in to say the bus is ready to transport people home. Obe is waiting for Holly and me, as he does most days now, as we often have a social excursion after the end of the day. Our parents are used to them, and by now they trust Obe. We also trust Obe. When he asks why the young miss is sad, Holly tells him about the murder. He is silent, and when he does talk he says only, "You all must be most careful." We ask him to take us to the Indian restaurant, Joyti. Obe declines to join us when we invite him and waits for us in his taxi. We order a light fare of pikoras and chai, and Holly says quietly, "This can't continue, Mason."

"I know, but I don't know what we can do."

"We can condemn it at least."

"Yes, but then what? A good number, maybe even a majority, of us are behind the killing of our adversaries. June's parents and now Cotton. None of them were very sympathetic characters, still ... maybe it's OK," I venture.

"No, it can't be. We're in danger of becoming as savage as so much of Typical society. We're smarter than they are. We have to be better."

57

Malcolm, Oklahoma

Shortly after Daniel's unilateral strike for justice, another issue raises its ugly head. Although the Attila Group is not a publicly traded company, we have garnered a fabulous amount of wealth, coming close to a top-100 company. We have deployed literally thousands of our people to accounting firms and money management activities. The head of this sector is overseen by John and Andrew. A good deal of our wealth is derived from the Rita water carafe and filter business, powered by the introduction of a benign form of cocaine added in small amounts to the replaceable cylinders. Sales are phenomenal, and we have cornered a good 85% of the market through scores of manufacturing and distribution plants throughout the country, beginning with our Maine operation. Building upon our successes, the Attila money group decides to expand our water empire to bottled drinking water. The group attempts to find a natural source of pure water and conducts concerted research into possible sources. This proves daunting, since so many possible sites are suffering from pollution—myriad crimes powered by ignorance and greed.

Finally, a potential site is found in a small town located at the mouth of a scenic canyon set astride both sides of a musical creek. The water is free of pollution and originates from underground aquifers located beneath the canyon. The town has a population of just about 700, and the canyon is owned privately by a rancher. Oklahoma is a corporate-friendly, pro-business state and welcomes us, anticipating taxes and potential jobs. We quickly buy the canyon and begin construction of the bottling plant. We pay attention not to alter the physical appearance of the creek or the canyon. While there is some machinery necessary to extracting the water, our main plant is built within the town and does little to alter the natural beauty of the landscape.

We are becoming adept at placing our people into communities where we locate our Rita factories. To do this, we use a small cadre of Typicals who are sympathetic to our goals and methods. These are recruited with care, well paid, discrete, and generally supportive of our cause. They initially orchestrate the interactions between townspeople, introduce our enterprise and people to the locals, and thus reduce the skepticism and biases directed against our workers and managers. As townspeople get used to seeing Mongoloids participate in society and running much of the business, the presence of the Typical facilitators is reduced, and they are moved to other sites. A few Typicals remain to buffer any awkward interactions. It has been our experience that as people get used to the way we look, they are free to move beyond their former biases and treat us as people.

The case of Malcolm, Oklahoma, is unique in a way for which we are unprepared. Malcolm is a religious community, homogenously composed of like-minded believers who follow a late-19th-century messiah named Malcolm. Malcolm's is a harsh and punitive theology, with strict and narrow interpretations of the Old Testament. Social rules and societal conduct is rigid, mediated by a single authority named Leroy. This is the only blemish to the otherwise pristine location of our first bottling plant.

The gene therapy program has conferred both intelligence and creative intellect to our members, fostering a great capacity to learn and analyze, but it does not initially provide any sophistication, nuance, or social savvy. In this way, our people are vulnerable to committing naive queries and responses. Our policy of keeping to ourselves and not demonstrating our intellect to Typicals has contributed to this naivete. The development of social sophistication is a steep learning curve, and this is exhibited outside a small grocery store in Malcolm. It comes from a simple exchange between Molly, a young woman new to our group, brought in to work in the bottling operation, and a young man named Caleb, a younger son of the religious leader—Leroy's offspring of half-siblings constitute a good 12 percent of the town's population.

Molly holds a grocery bag of food waiting to be picked up by a van that will take her to her cabin. She had previously seen Caleb at the plant. Unknown to Molly, Caleb had been discharged from the water plant for his imperious attitude and language directed toward his Mongoloid coworkers. Caleb is not the first to be dismissed for prejudiced and overtly hostile behavior by a townsperson toward a worker or manager; it is here where our Typical buffers earn their keep. Local hostility is becoming more of a problem in Malcolm than it has been in any of our other locations. We have been forced to remain vigilant and continue to monitor the situation closely. Molly knew little of this, and nothing of Caleb's acrimonious history. I base this account on a written firsthand report provided by Molly's roommate, Sarah, who was in the store on unrelated business and overheard the interaction.

Making conversation, Molly asked: "Did you come here before there was a town?"

"Yeah," Caleb answered petulantly, "we founded this town. Named it— built everything."

Molly had studied the history of the civil rights movement, as had all Attilians, and it's here she commits her fatal *faux pas*. "Was the town named after Malcolm X?" she asked, casually summoning up the only Malcolm she knows.

"What?" erupted Caleb with surprise and aggression. "I should say NOT, if you think that anyone here would honor that nigger, you don't even belong here." With that, Caleb turns and leaves the nonplussed young woman to ruminate on the shocking word he used in his response.

Religious cults, as that what Malcolm was, have always been suspicious of outsiders, which we are. Caleb went immediately to his father with tales of godlessness and the impending danger our group posed as the spearhead of a Black takeover that threatened to destroy the Malcolm way of life. Now the ambient suspicion had a focus.

Leader Leroy, already antagonistic toward the outsiders, needed little convincing and called a town meeting at the wood-slatted church in the center of town along the east side of the creek. As is typical of such meetings, it continued late into the night.

58

Molly's End

Sarah continues the tale in her own words:

I am concerned with the conversation I overhear between Molly and the leader's son, and I decide to hang back and do some follow-up observation. I follow Caleb to his father's house and station myself just outside of the picket fence surrounding the small front yard; their voices are excited, and I can hear the substance of their exchange.

Caleb tells his father that he's found out that the water group is a front for a Black takeover that aims to model the town after the teachings of Malcolm X, impose its godless rules, and enslave its inhabitants. The Leader, Leroy, reacts furiously, shouting invectives directed toward us corrupt outsider mutations, and I can hear the banging of cabinets and drawers as Leroy prepares his next actions.

I move one house away and continue to observe as the leader and his son exit the house, and I proceed hurriedly to their church a short distance away near the center of town. The bell is rung and the townspeople quickly fill the wooden structure. Only men are allowed to attend, but even so, the church quickly fills with perhaps 100 or more crowded around the open double doors of the church.

It's late afternoon and the light is fading, and I move to the outskirts of the crowd but close enough to hear the Leader. Leroy rails: "These outsider mutations have seized our canyon, stolen our water, and want to transform it into a home for nigger followers of the godless Malcolm X, turning us all into slaves, to serve them." With flailing arms and rising voice, he shouts, "Our very way of life is threatened—do you want to let that happen?" His words and dramatic gestures further insight his xenophobic parishioners into a frenzied mob of increasing fear and hostility; during his harangue they emit a constant stream of guttural outrage. As long as Leader Leroy's screed continues, the outside group of faithfuls are focused on the open doors, but as the church disbands, proceeding from rhetoric toward action, the group turns and sees one of the mutants in their mix and converge on me, pinning me to the wall of the church, saying "she's one of 'um," waiting for instructions before they move further against me. At this point, the leader and his son exit the building into the crowd and Caleb sees me. "That's not her," he says, in an uncharacteristic magnanimous gesture that the crowd takes as permission to release me. Their minds are small but their focus is narrow, and I am freed from looming disaster, and I drift to the periphery but continue to observe.

The mob, brandishing the obligatory torches and armed with wooden spreaders used to support the wire between barbed-wire fence poles, seeks the location of the small house where Molly resides in the little clusters of rustic cabins that have been built to house the workers at the various water extraction points, moving up the ridge of the canyon. We live in the furthest house up the ridge.

By the light of their torches, brandishing their narrow wooden clubs, the mob moves up the canyon, knocking on doors at random. A number of Attilians seek to oppose the mob, both male and female workers place themselves between the mob and their direction up the creek, but they are overpowered by superior numbers; some receive blows from the wooden fence posts and barrel staves carried by the enraged citizens. It is testimony to the single-mindedness of mob followers that none of the brave workers are killed—again, the result of small minds and narrow focus. Chants of death "to the nigger lover," and "mutants will not replace us" fill the air astride the flames of the torches. Some of the cabins are set on fire from the torches of the crazed hunters. I continue to follow.

"They've come for Molly," defenders shout to their comrades, and in this way the mob learns the name of their quarry. Chants are then modified to "Death to Molly" as they move inexorably up the slope of the canyon. Molly shares a cabin with with me and one other woman; it is situated on the farthermost extraction point of the canyon. Neighbors from farther down slow the process of the mob and warn the confused Molly of her impending danger.

Molly's other roommate, Barbra, is at home with her and continues the story:

Despite Molly's peril she remains relatively calm and analytical, reviewing her history, trying to identify the transgression that's mushroomed into the present danger. "But I've done nothing to anger these people," says Molly, trying to make sense of the situation. "I need to talk to them to explain I meant no harm—no threat."

I'm more agitated than she is. "No! You have to get out of here, they're coming for you," I implore her. "Get out now, and I'll tell them that you're not here." The fire from the torches is continuing to move up the ridge and the chants of "Death to Molly" can be clearly heard. She flees the house in growing fear and incomprehension.

Sarah continues the narrative:

I had worked my way up behind the vanguard of the group as they reach Molly's cabin, and I can hear Barbra saying that Molly isn't home. A member of the mob spots her as she vacates the house through the back door.

"There she goes," he says to the assembly of pursuers, "after her," and his fellows rush to follow. She can see the light from the advancing mob flow around her house and up the slope ever closer. I watch as Molly scrambles up the rugged ridge that leads to the summit; I imagine her fingernails broken and bleeding, bruises forming on her forearms, shins, and knees. The water in the creek below thunders through the canyon, drowning out the cries of the mob. The canyon wall becomes too steep to scramble up as it nears the peak; Molly is trapped and turns to face the mob as it converges. Despite all that has happened, Molly seems composed as she steps back onto the ledge of the canyon, and her mouth is moving though all I can hear is the water. Then I see her go over the side.

Accounts differ, even between the pursuers in their subsequent testimony. Even I can't tell. She is either pushed off the side by her assailants, falls, or hurls herself into the creek below. Whatever the case, Molly dies at the hands of a mob instigated by fear and hatred, as does Frankenstein's monster in a horror movie I once saw.

Whatever the truth of her last moments, the result is a barely recognizable young dead woman found in the creek, washed up onto an outcropping of rocks at the mouth of the canyon.

59

John Has His Say and Amy Has a Plan

The police, located a good 50 miles away in Avery, are called. They have a policy of not entering the unpredictable Malcolm at night, and arrive by mid-morning the following day to find a dead Mongoloid woman, bruised and beaten Attilian workers, and a few burned structures. People are interviewed, forms completed, but no charges are filed.

When we hear the news, a ruling council is called. The ruling council, as it is now referred to, was formed from the fifteen original members of the gene therapy study plus Matthew, and it gathers in the large room we have redesigned as a rough amphitheater. Early in our history, we made our decisions by consensus, with everyone in the group needing to be in agreement. This superior form of leadership has since ceded to an inferior majority rule policy to deal with the appearance of rising differences expressed within the group, reflecting the growing diversity of its members as they become more individualistic in their thinking and outlook. This change in our previous equanimity was originally inspired by Holly, whose highly developed sense of moral integrity often injected itself into our decisions as a lone voice of opposition at the expense of efficiency. In our last exercise of consensus, we vote Matthew to the periphery, as a non-voting member, in order to have an odd number of votes, and we institute majority rule.

On the news and subsequent reports of Malcolm, we are outraged, confused, and edgy as we began our meeting. Matthew is there to take notes. Much talk and adamant conversations between pairs and small groups occurs as John stands up to speak. John has become the harshest critic of Typicals and Typical society, supplanting Charles. "This is intolerable," he begins. "But it's consistent with the attitudes we are confronted with by Typicals, and it demands action." Here, he looks directly at Daniel, who nods back at him. We all take his meaning. "The police have lodged no charges or even taken steps to seriously investigate it as a crime, treating it as an accident, even though structures were burned and our members beaten. It is what we should expect from Typicals." I look at the group and almost everyone is nodding. Holly looks at me anxiously, frozen in place. John continues: "I say we have served them as victims for too long and need to extract justice. This has not been the first time we have been put in danger by people with rigid and hateful religious beliefs." He looks at June, who nods.

John has advocated retribution on Typical society before and was the strongest advocate of Daniel's killing of the Congressman. So far, actions that he and others proposed have been voted down through Holly's arguments and the group's good sense. Amy, who has increasingly allied herself with John and his positions, stands to speak. "I have thought about this since I was informed of the tragedy, and I have a plan to eradicate the whole damn town." Holly looks at me and mouths "No." Now it's I who sit frozen.

Amy continues: "I agree with John, it's time to take action, and I believe the whole community bears some responsibility for the crime. Look, I've done some research and studied aerial photos; the whole town's water is derived from the creek running through it and is stored in one water tower. It will be easy enough to inject a modified gene therapy agent into the water system along with a rare benign bacterium. It's a strategy similar to the red tide algae we used with June's parents, which will show up in the autopsies of the fatalities. The gene therapy agent will do the job, and the benign bacterium will take the blame. The gene therapy chemicals are not on anyone's radar screen and the bacterium will be recognized. Our people, particularly our Typical facilitators, should avoid drinking town water, but Mongoloids can drink it with impunity. My proposal to the group is to send a small cadre of our people to execute the plan. Safety for our Typicals can be further protected through the administration of a small dose of a modified and weakened gene therapy agent that functions as a vaccine; it will act as a buffer against larger doses of the gene therapy agent, conferring a virtual immunity." With that, Amy, the architect of the transformation of literally millions of Mongoloids, sits down docilely.

Holly is instantly on her feet. "There are innocent people that will die as a result of this. Children..."

John immediately responds, "This is true, but it is the whole town that is a threat to all of us. The police could have taken steps to find the guilty and ensure our safety, but they have negated their responsibility and it's up to us to take action." I look around the group and most of the heads are nodding and stating words of support.

Holly, still on her feet, makes the final plea. "We need to be better than they are."

John responds, "We are better than they are. Unless the police take some appropriate action, I vote we adopt Amy's plan." When a few days later the police have taken no action, the group votes 12 to 3 to execute Amy's plan. The dissenters are Holly, me, and, of all people, Logan, who says echoing a phrase used against Native Americans, "So, the only good Malcolmian is a dead Malcolomian? Fuckin' A, I sure do miss consensus."

A small team of the biochemical group led by Amy is deployed to Malcolm—the logistics are painfully facile. The water tower is breached, and the toxic chemical cocktail is inserted—people begin their death throes almost immediately. The deaths are similar to those of Dr. Malone's staff, Tim and Theresa, and are probably just as painful, though much quicker. Within two days, the whole town, along with the cult of Malcolm, is gone. Amy has sharpened her skills; the local police were as effective in solving the murder of the town as they were in solving Molly's.

That's how we came to murder a whole town. Our murder count is now up to 703: the whole of Malcolm, Oklahoma (not one survivor), June's parents, and the Congressman exploded by Daniel. The world may be better off without these souls, but we are not. I think this act changes the Attila Group fundamentally and leads to our next phase.

In a final bit of cynicism, the group votes to name the water company Malcolm Water, like the name on a tombstone, ironically honoring the creator of the religious cult that killed Molly.

Attilians had discovered black humor.

Profile: John

John assumed prominence in our group as a member of Charles' technical and financial group and quickly distinguished himself with his knowledge of financial institutions and quick mind for entrepreneurial projects and interventions. Along with Andrew, he was the originator and driver of many of our financial successes. His parents both came from old-money families whose only vocation in life was managing their assets, voting Republican, and championing conservative causes. At his time of birth, both of John's parents were in late middle age; John came as an afterthought and remained so throughout his childhood and youth.

They were content to place their son in a series of elite boarding schools and take leave of their parental responsibility. John later described his education as a mosaic of nonsense and isolation. The schools favored privileged boys from wealthy families, whose only disability consisted of a dearth of empathy, and John was teased mercilessly. Little academic accommodation was made to his special needs as a learner, as the administration remained content to cash John's father's generous donation checks.

John writes:

> *"As I sat quietly in the back of the classroom, my loneliness hardened to cynicism, then to anger, and finally to hatred. I truly hated the other boys, and resolved that one day I would take revenge, though I had no conception of how. Revenge, however, transformed into resignation as each day passed into another. Holidays were the worst, my parent's condescension more odious than the humiliations of my classmates. When the gene replacement therapy kicked in, I had words for my anguish, and I resolved never again to let society enter my life. The Attilians gave me an outlet. I see it as an opportunity to wall off society, and like the*

proverbial little Dutch boy, keep the dyke plugged against any and all intrusions."

It was this history of experiences that permanently wounded this otherwise kind and creative soul. As John matured, his early hatreds were replaced by a certain productive pragmatism to dealing with problems. Although our collective response to Malcolm more than settled his debt, John seemed to derive no pleasure from the act.

60

Attila Discovers Spirituality

Five years after our first meeting with Dr. Malone, Bad Mr. 21's killer, Holly and I are 18. Adults, with no guardians to determine our lives and future. As a result of Amy's augmented gene therapy, the distribution of the Rita water system, an outreach program of early home care for Mongoloid toddlers, and special schools and programs, the only un-transformed Mongoloids left are infants. Our Rita water filter plants have been co-opted for use in manufacturing significant amounts of the gene therapy agent—other plants have been established worldwide—and the number of Standards is dwindling. We continue to communicate with Holly's system of reading between the letters, in the form of simple emails and children's books and stories. It is amazing the degree to which Mongoloids can keep a secret, and while certain suspicions are raised from time to time, our anonymity is so far preserved.

The murder of Malcolm, now a year in the past, however, has shaken our groups across the globe, engendering a diversity of opinions, that threaten to split us apart and violate our previous cohesion. We are so large a group these days that we outnumber some small countries. To manage and coordinate our programs, there are currently 1,576 regional councils similar to our ruling council, and we have heard from all of them with their reactions to Malcolm. Sentiment seems roughly equal, for and against. From European Union countries where capital punishment is outlawed, the sentiment is decidedly against. African councils lean slightly to the for. Asia is about equal. Australia, although a small population, is the country most against by percentage if not by total number. American councils are the most supportive. The total numbers are roughly equal. The level of invective is a new experience for us and we seem a far cry from consensus. And with no clear agreement, the conversations remain spirited, passionate, and sometimes bellicose.

Holly is despondent in the wake of the discord, and most often morose in our evening conversations. We have moved in together and leased a small apartment across from a quiet park in the Adams-Morgan section of D.C., within walking distance of our Indian restaurant. We could have moved closer to the university but we would have sacrificed our travel time with Obe, who has become an important part of our lives and a touchstone for Holly. Our new living situation was quite the adjustment for our parents. My father, particularly, has had a hard time, but to his credit acclimated to the situation. My mother, characteristically, was proud in the end. Nighttime is the hardest for Holly, but days are not much better, reacting to her colleagues with a combination of sadness and disbelief. I begin to worry about her intractable dark moods and try to draw her focus to positive aspects of our work, and to our lives in general. When queried about her mood, she only shakes her head and says, "I thought we were better than this," then falls silent.

As a group, we have pretty much rejected organized religion in favor of a varied and eclectic philosophy. Many of us come with family backgrounds in Christianity, which we almost unanimously dismiss as shot through with logical contradictions; studies of Judaism and Islam do little to bridge the logical discrepancies. Thus, most of us could be categorized as atheists, not agnostics, since for the majority of us, our analysis is complete. Instead, we substitute a loose empirical hodgepodge of moral principles that, in the end, is a collection of the experiences of each individual. So far, that's been enough.

Since my earliest forays into understanding Mongolism, when I came up against the confusing reference of Mongolians, I have maintained an interest in Mongolian history and culture.

Attila, our patronymic, it turns out was quite liberal in his acceptance of religions. He himself embraced Tengriism, a shamanistic religion characterized by animism and totemism, but he was tolerant of other religions. I became interested in Buddhism when I read about the debate as to whether it was a religion or philosophy. I read a number of books and came down on the philosophy side of the argument. I was struck by the injunction to test everything through one's own experience, not accepting anything through authority. There is no retreat to soul or heaven, or the panacea of grace. If you accepted nirvana as a psychological state and rebirth and karma as a collective responsibility extending past the grave, take-it-all-around (as Huck Finn might say) it was primarily a functional system of empirical psychology. In my reading, I was particularly taken by the writings and approach of the current Dalai Lama. I did further research on him, read everything he'd ever written, and discovered that he was doing a public teaching in two weeks in Paris. I went online and bought tickets that had been sold out for months, but a few were offered by individuals at an extreme markup. I didn't care and bought two on the spot. I also didn't consult Holly. We were going.

61

Thu Je Che

Holly is particularly despondent as Daniel has struck again, using his same MO of explosives in parking garages. "I'll need to change things up the next time so that the police don't notice a Mongoloid youth walking away from parking garage murders," he says, not sugarcoating anything. His victim was another southern Congressman who had publicly derided a young immigrant mother and her Mongoloid child who had been abused by immigration officials—Congress 0, Daniel 2. Deep in chronic depression, Holly offers little resistance to the Paris trip and seems to be moderately distracted by the idea of it. Ever the linguist, she focuses her time on learning Tibetan.

We leave from Reagan International Airport, named after a now senile friend of my father's. Predictably, we are greeted with suspicion—two Mongoloids traveling without a chaperone. We are pulled out of line and interrogated by TSA staff for fifteen minutes or so until we convince the authorities that we possess adequate intellect and awareness to sit in our seats for six hours without causing mayhem or safety threats. "We dare not share this experience with Daniel," I quip to Holly. I regret saying this when she just shakes her head sadly.

When we arrive in France, few people react to our Mongolism. Parisians are said to be unfriendly, but we don't find this so and are greeted with smiles as we speak their language, Holly flawlessly. This attitude extends beyond the airport to our hotel and restaurants, where although possibly curious, people all have the good manners not to make our extra chromosome an issue. And the food is lovely.

The venue for the four-day teaching is in a turn-of-the-century opera house that is a splendid piece of architecture. Our Internet ticket sellers have placed us behind a pillar that somewhat obstructs our view of the stage. The Dalai Lama notices us trying to adapt—I think he had tracked us from our entry, and he invites us to take VIP seats up front. We gladly occupy them, and when we are close enough for him to hear, Holly says clearly, "Thu je che," thank you in Tibetan. To which he laughs raucously and presses his palms together in a namaste and bows his head to Holly, who returns the courtesy. Over the four days in our VIP seats, Holly's darkness melts into sunshine. We both have read all of his books, but it is his personality that really captivates us. Holly, over a lovely dinner at a street-side café, says enthusiastically, "It is his compassion, his logical and intelligent spirituality, all mediated through his humor, that is so effective—it's like, like spiritual vitamins." She giggles for the first time in a long while. Then she says seriously, "I wish that I could bottle it and take it back to the group."

We stay two extra days in Paris and do the tourist thing, the Eiffel Tower, the Louvre, the Notre Dame Cathedral, and return home with Holly resolving to bring spirituality to the Attilians, to bottle it in fact. She immediately calls a group meeting where she outlines the possible benefits of Buddhist practice, and is received well—she is given the go-ahead to develop an in-house workshop.

In it, she makes the point that intellect is largely an internal enterprise, composed of many inner conversations, events, and revelations. Understanding is its major reinforcement, with no external rewards necessary. After hiding our abilities from Typicals all these years, we are used to this quiet, albeit sometime stressful, monologue. Holly's prescription for meditation sets us free. It catches us by surprise and sweeps through us like fire. It is meditation:

walking, seated, standing, riding in the bus, washing the dishes, that provides the context for the principles addressed initially by Holly's workshop. She puts together a system of Buddhism that strips out all of the cultural and doctrinaire trappings. This approach is strictly philosophical; a call to testing every aspect of life through one's own experience, and to live not in the past or future, but in the reality of where one exists in the present. The revelations provided by this philosophy and the technique of meditation are almost as transformative as gene therapy itself, such that mindfulness comes to compete with intellect in an internal battle in all of us, which would become a paramount factor in our collective future.

Phase VI

The End So Far

62

Strong Corrective Action

This internal state of mindfulness, while contributing to a peace of mind, competes with external pressures of daily life and struggles against the isolationists' agenda for dominance. Of all the members of the ruling council, John suffers the most. As the strongest advocate for a dramatic culling of the worldwide Typical population, he finds the emphasis on self-reflection and compassion confounding. Daniel, whose internal dialogue is as inactive as is his outer communication, continues his assault on the members of Congress he finds pernicious. While many of us disagree with his actions, none disagree with his targets, so he keeps up his program of modifying the congressional landscape. The FBI forms a special task force to investigate the House murders, and this only seems to animate Daniel's actions, as he varies his locations and contexts, but not his delivery which employs direct participation and detonation with a burner phone, and incorporates zero tolerance of collateral damage. Our murders of individuals now inch toward eight.

John continues to wrestle with his morality and compassion on one side, and the logic of what he feels is the appropriate direction for both our group's and the world's future on the other. He writes a number of articles for our global newsletter articulately outlining his dilemma, highlighting what all of us are all experiencing. But it is Daniel who provides an unlikely solution. By this time, most of us have read a number of books by the Dalai Lama, but it is Daniel's viewing of an online video that provides John his breakthrough. In a video interview, the Dalai Lama is asked how his notions of compassion toward all people can be used to combat evil in society and initiate social change. He answers that adherence to this principle does not preclude engagement in what he refers to as strong corrective action—indeed, it demands it. There it was: *Strong Corrective Action* solved the conflict, at least for John, by marrying compassion with what John felt was the logical approach to saving the planet, and ourselves, through a program of strong corrective action, executed by a culling of 90 percent of the Typical population. John immediately writes an article laying out the theory, logic, morality, and pragmatism behind it. This causes an instant sensation with Mongoloids around the world and throws our group into chaos. Strong corrective action becomes a cry, not only for a philosophy but also for a course of action. The debate between the advocates of strong corrective action and those advocating a gentler approach rages for over a year and threatens to break us apart.

John and his adherents point out that Molly's murder represents an impending threat, a tragedy that will happen again. Adherents also highlight the impact of practices Typical society impose on the environment and endangered species. This last argument moves even Holly, who grapples miserably with her conscience. We now have more money than God, as is the saying, and contribute to organizations that advocate for responsible environmental, educational, and economic practices. We even hire a few lobbyists to advocate for endangered species and Holly's beloved elephants, but with negligible results. What we see as the wrong-headed intractability of Typicals to execute responsible scientific, social, and economic policies fuels a good deal of our angst. That, in turn, provides sentiment for the strong-corrective-action camp. Amy and her group begin working globally on vaccines that would confer immunity to favored Typicals, thus protecting them against our chosen means of mass murder. It is now two years since the killings in Malcolm—things threaten to explode.

63

Reproduction

Ethical decisions aside, there are a number of problems that need to be resolved before we could institute our program of culling all but ten percent of the Typical population. With the rise in popularity of strong corrective action, the practical question becomes: How do we maintain our population over time? And the biggest question is reproduction.

Ninety-nine percent of Mongoloids are born to Typicals. Only recently have a number of Mongoloids been the result of births between Mongoloids. Historically, there has been a prejudice against letting us breed or to even engage in sex. This is true even in progressive settings where Mongoloid marriage is allowed, both birth control and sterilization are frequent. It has only been lately that some Mongoloid couples have pioneered families.

The discussion is two-pronged: functional and aesthetic. Our group is relatively young, but this is not true for all the global councils currently grappling with these issues in their own way. As I am telling this story from my perspective and I'm asked, as the Mongoloid expert, to provide an explanation; this is mine. Amy probably could do a better job, but I'll do my best to address the issue.

Although I have addressed some of the technical issues of Down Syndrome in a few places throughout my narrative, I provide a review here for the indulgent reader. Functionally, Mongolism is caused by an extra chromosome in those affected. It's termed trisomy 21, or three number 21 chromosomes in all, or most, Mongoloid cells. Humans typically have one pair of 23 distinctive chromosomes. Chromosome pairs are numbered by size, and thus genetic material, with 1 being the largest. Autosomes (or body chromosomes) are those numbered 1 to 22, with 22 being the smallest. As I've stated before, Mongoloids actually have three chromosomes 22 not three 21s, but in the history of medical literature the term was established and maintained, choosing convenience over veracity. The last pair represents the sex chromosomes termed X and Y that determine the gender of each individual. Each cell of the body contains a full complement of 46 chromosomes, 23 from the mother, 23 from the father.

The process of reducing cells of 46 chromosomes, 23 pairs, to 23 individual chromosomes is termed "reductional division," or "meiosis." Somewhere in this reductional process, one gamete (sperm or egg) gets two chromosome 22s rather than just one, and when joined to an unaffected gamete the result is three 22s, producing a Mongoloid individual. (The sequence is slightly different for Mosaics, in whom the process occurs somewhere in development.)

So, what does all this have to do with the strong-corrective-action movement? Well, if you remove 90 percent of Typicals and 99 percent of Mongoloids are born to Typical mothers, aren't we ensuring our extinction? The answer is a reassuring "not necessarily," since when mongoloids breed with each other there are four possible outcomes, three that are viable, and roughly proportional. A zygote (or fertilized egg) from which a new individual is created can have two complements of trisomy 22 for a total of four chromosome 22s, in which case the zygote is not viable and is naturally aborted, a 25 percent chance; it could be composed of one typical gamete and one trisomy 22, in which the individual would be viable and Mongoloid; this outcome occurs at roughly 50 percent. Or it could be made up of a typical gamete from each Mongoloid parent, resulting in a Typical offspring, and this is roughly a 25 percent chance. Thus, despite the genetic probabilities, a viable baby would either be Mongoloid or Typical, and these numbers would secure the populations of both Mongoloids and of Typicals. Though not commensurate with Typical couplings, it would structure for a rebuilding of the diminished Typical population. It is argued that Typicals born to and raised by Mongoloid parents would be more intelligent, compassionate, and less destructive to the planet. This is good news to a number of fence-sitters.

The aesthetic consideration concerns our increasing confidence and independence as a worldwide group. With our growing self-awareness is a new appreciation of our Attilian brothers and sisters as desirable mates. We naturally begin to view each other as attractive, rather than as a mutation of a desired type. With this perspective, our "Mongoloid is Beautiful" phase is born.

64

Three Choices

The stress of determining our future trajectory is affecting relationships between us, both as individuals and as groups. Strong advocates on each of the sides compete acrimoniously for dominance, and it is now clear that something has to be done to restore our previous cohesion. The answer comes from a council in Sweden, which first calls for a worldwide binding vote of all Mongoloids to determine a consistent future direction. The next part is a little more difficult—to decide exactly what we are voting on.

The elephant in the room is Strong Corrective Action, which calls for the extinction of a good 90 percent of Typicals. The list in favor of this option is long: inept and corrupt stewardship of our planet, exploitation of environmental and economic resources, Typicals' propensity for wars, unequal distribution of wealth, the prejudiced treatment of vulnerable people by the powerful, mindless extinction of plant and animal species, pollution of oceans, air, and fresh water, and the rapacious use of land and natural resources. All militate for the drastic reduction of the offending population. This direction is carried by a strong logic that is hard to deny. It is both a pragmatic, and draconian, strategy, and from the outset, this path seems to garner the strongest support.

The second option is less internally consistent than is Strong Corrective Action, and comprises two distinct strategies. The first is to continue with the current system of already instituted policies and projects. These include contributions to sympathetic and progressive organizations, the funding of special advocates (read lobbyists), and the not-insignificant influence we have on Typical society simply through our participation with a new competence, independence and confidence. The second component of this strategy is more radical and calls for the creation and institution of shadow governments funded and managed by us. This comes from the American revelation that it is money, provided to legislators and other bureaucrats by the powerful, that determines the direction of government and society. This tendency is even stronger in less democratic regimes. The logic is that we have the money, and it is time to be powerful. This strategy takes its nickname from a Beatles song and is termed "Let It Be." Besides, Daniel was already making inroads with his one-man modification campaign of Congress. This was the choice, sans Daniel, that was initially most attractive to Holly and me.

Then there appears a third alternative.

65

Mongoloid and Proud

The third option is really a variant of the of second, but with a twist. It became known as "Mongoloid and Proud."This option also called for a maintenance of the status quo, with a continuation of our programs and projects: a continuation of the worldwide gene therapy program, support for our communication systems, education, schools, residential programs, and programs of health and nutrition. Although there seemed little difference between this strategy and the second, of Let it Be, the third choice then took a surprising departure, calling for a return to the social roles occupied by Mongoloids in our previous histories before gene therapy. This option was given the mocking name "Mongoloid and Proud." Up to this time, embedded in all our programs was the progressive notion that we would be remaking society to more equitably include Mongoloids in all of its aspects and institutions and gradually emerging from our self-imposed cocoons into full citizenship, where our superior intellects could be fully acknowledged, if not actually embraced. Rather than viewing Mongoloids as agents of direct social change, "Mongoloid and Proud" seemed to call for a retreat back into our previous situation and status. The leaders of this movement, for that was what it had become, quickly emphasized that it was indeed a retreat to a similar situation, at least on the surface, but not to a previous status. In effect, we would continue our work, but from the fringes.

With our financial resources and infrastructure, we already controlled the means of education and social support for Mongoloids globally. Movement leaders argued that our situation had advanced dramatically. One needed only to look to the success of our poverty reduction measures to see the gains in the lives of Mongoloids and their families. These leaders also invoked the new spirituality and its meditation techniques as a means to rise above the prejudices of individuals and the biases of society, and within our own minds and existing networks lead internally meaningful, productive, and creative lives.

Members of the "Mongoloid and Proud" contingent, now fully embracing its ironic sobriquet, are quick to say that the approach is only a strategy. A strategy whereby Mongoloids place themselves as a focal point around which society is allowed to evolve, but along fully humane and nonviolent principles, while influencing progressive policies and decisions. The group states that "to kill 90 percent of Typicals is a social wrong that will destroy our own internal integrity and morality and, in the end, diminish our legitimacy."

The "Mongoloid and Proud" advocates close their arguments with the pragmatic statement that Mongoloids worldwide will remain free to use the other options in the future if the Mongoloid and Proud option proves ineffective, but that it should be tried first. From its original reception of ridicule, "Mongoloid and Proud" was gaining support.

We spend a year defining, discussing, and debating these three options. Finally, a vote is imminent. The next months are used to finalize the ballot and set out procedures for the global vote. Holly authored a statement that was included in the ballot, stating essentially that whatever the final vote, it in no way restricts the rights of individuals to pursue their own lives and determine their own destinies. The die was cast.

66

Night

It is night in Africa. Holly and I have relocated to Nigeria. We purchased two thousand acres from Obe's cousin, one of his many cousins who are ubiquitous throughout all the continent. The land adjoins a medium-sized elephant preserve to which we have allied ourselves, funding a large anti-poaching program that employs a couple of hundred locals, as many hand-held radios, a fleet of Land Rovers, and a helicopter. Currently, we are negotiating to buy a large tract of land that will increase the size of the park to a half-million acres. Obe has abandoned his taxi service and made the move along with us to become our head man, major domo, and trusted friend. He has proved himself a master negotiator.

He still calls Holly Young Miss, but all others here call her Young Mistress, and me they call Master. Our physical characters don't seem to be infected by the biases of home, and we labor under no preconceived limitations, except sometimes with white Western visitors, but they are dispelled of their notions quickly, sans the oppressive trappings of our native country, by our demeanor.

Tonight, the votes will be cast that determine the fate and direction of Mongoloid society, and the fate of Typical society as well. There are twenty million Mongoloids worldwide taking part in the vote that will be binding for our group as a whole, though not for each of us as individuals. We have managed a pure democracy: Every one of our twenty million souls has access to a laptop, if not a laptop itself. We have safeguards against people voting more than once, though Mongoloids, as a general rule, seem incapable of cheating. So, we wait expectantly for the outcome. Holly and I are at the whim of time zones; we will know the result of the vote by noon tomorrow.

It's nine o'clock where we are, the sun hesitates, debating its final descent into darkness; the birds have ceased their chatter, believing in the inevitability of night—the night sounds have yet to fully awaken. I look at Holly across the yard, the only sound is the rustling of the elephants in the rehabilitation pens. We are alone now. "What do you think will happen?" she asks. The question is mostly rhetorical, but it prompts me to review the options before us.

1. Culling of nine tenths of the Typical population as a strategy to preserve the homeostasis of the planet and all species on it. We've become quite accomplished assassins. 2. Maintaining our present trajectory of economic influence, social and educational programs supported through our newfound spirituality, this punctuated by occasional murders. 3. A strategic, de facto retreat into traditional Mongoloid roles, though not status.

Holly and I have agonized over our decisions and, in the end, both decided to vote for the second option with all of its flaws, though not without a serious consideration of "Mongoloid and Proud." Holly particularly was drawn to the "Mongoloid and Proud" logic and strategy, but she made her final decision on what she thought was best for her elephants, feeling that the Let it Be option would deploy more resources to their preservation. I argued that if elephants were the final consideration, Strong Corrective Action would be the most effective. Holly agreed and suffered her choice.

After my ruminations, I answer her question as to what will happen. "I don't think I know which of the three choices is best. It won't matter for us in the short run."

"Mason, 90 percent of Typicals. ... How will we choose? How can we ever justify it?"

"Ya pays your money, and ya takes your chances," I unwisely quip, and she slaps me hard. It is the first act of violence I have ever seen Holly commit, and I am chastened for my insensitive remark. But both my comment and Holly's response are indications of the stress we feel. I take the offending hand and hold it, and Holly kisses me on the cheek. The African night sounds are in full-throated chorus, and we are left to sleep fitfully and await the African noon.

67

Day

To the members of Typical society I would like to say to you, "You're safe for now, but the next time you find yourself in the presence of a Mongoloid, maybe bagging your groceries or stacking produce in the vegetable section of your market, manning a broom and dustpan, vacantly smiling at a baseball game, look them in the face beyond their slanty eyes, odd-shaped head, and good natured distant smile, and into the being that resides inside, and realize that they are a dike holding back a sea that could drown you and yours in an eye blink." I would like to say this to you, but I can't. For I am Mongoloid and Proud, and have to go take care of the elephants.

Afterword

Caution.

Acknowledgments

To the persons critical to the support and ultimate publication of this book. To Andrea Peacock, who edited the manuscript and provided both expertise and encouragement to the author. To Sidney W. Bijou, mentor throughout my career in special education and behavioral psychology, who stuck with his intractable student to the end. To Doug Peacock, who read the manuscript and provided valuable critique in the sculpting of the narrative. To William Halloran of the Department of Education, who was there throughout all my adventures with government. To Jon Kulczycki for his precise reading and subtle suggestions. To Ned Gittings, who provided the sensitive cover illustration, and gave Mason Free a face. And finally, to Craig Lancaster for fashioning the book into its final form. Thanks to one and all.

About the author

Jamey Gittings holds a Ph.D. in special education and rehabilitation, with an emphasis in behavioral psychology from the University of Arizona, with minor areas in anthropology and genetics. He has served in teaching and research positions in the Department of Special Education and Rehabilitation, and was a Research Director for the Arizona State Museum in the Department of Anthropology. He has served as an occasional instructor in the department of Special Education and Rehabilitation. He has founded a school for youth and adults with a variety of disabilities, including Down Syndrome. And has written and directed a federal grant program from the U.S. Department of Education, Office of Special Education and Rehabilitative Services, similar to the one presented in this book.

www.ingramcontent.com/pod-product-compliance
Lightning Source LLC
Chambersburg PA
CBHW032009050726
47590CB00006B/2106